THE
SIREN
AND THE
SCHOLAR

❧❦❧

FARAWAY CASTLE

THE SIREN AND THE SCHOLAR
Faraway Castle Book 2

THE

SIREN

AND THE

SCHOLAR

FARAWAY CASTLE

J.M. STENGL

OTHER BOOKS BY J.M. STENGL

FARAWAY CASTLE

NOVELLAS
Cinder Ellie
The Little Siren

NOVELS
The Siren and the Scholar
The Rose and the Briar
The Lady and the Wish
The Mirror and the Curse

A VILLAIN'S EVER AFTER

The Baker and the Wolf

To Jenelle H.,
first a client, now my friend,
encourager, and prayer-partner.
Blessings on your own writing journey!

1

WHAT IS HAPPENING *to me?*
Sunlight fell in beams through the roiling green water around me, bubbles rising to the surface as I flailed about. I was in my own lake but frightened and confused and . . . My tail! Oh, such pain—as if someone took a knife and split me from my tail fins upward. I screamed, but there was no sound. Nobody was around to hear me anyway, not even any fish. No one came to help me. I thrashed and fought, but there was no one to fight.

"Mother!" I cried. I thought I sensed her near, but I heard no answer.

My familiar surroundings seemed blurred and foreign. Then I tried to breathe and choked on water. Wait, what? Why couldn't I breathe like always?

My body had changed; I knew it now. My tail was no longer a tail, and it felt different. The lake water against my skin felt cold because I had no scales anymore. I had bare skin on my lower half too, like a human, and something wrapped around my hips.

Not being able to breathe was terrifying! Pulling with my arms and kicking a little with my new legs, which didn't go very well, I reached the surface and coughed until I could suck in a long breath without choking. It had never felt so good to breathe air before, and the blue sky above was a comfort after the cold, threatening green depths of . . . my home.

Oh, this was *so* not good. And I had no idea whatsoever why it was happening to me.

Paddling with my arms and hands, I turned to locate myself. I floated in a northeast bay of Faraway Lake, still within sight of the castle, but far enough away that the people on the beach and docks looked like grains of sand. A ski boat approached slowly; I saw three human faces staring directly at me. That was a shock, since humans can't usually see me unless I speak to them. Staff members at the castle can see magical beings like me, since they have a little magic of their own. But the guests? Almost never.

I couldn't truly be human, could I? I mean, I was born a siren, and everything I knew about life was from my merfolk perspective.

Mother did this—she turned me into a human. She must have. But why? What have I done to deserve having my tail chopped in half and being nearly drowned in my own home? I was terrified and angry and shivering with cold, and wet hair plastered my face and shoulders.

"Are you all right?" The voice sounded feminine.

"What happened to you?" another female asked.

"Strange to see a girl out here alone in the lake." That was a deep voice edged with amusement. "She doesn't look like she's drowning."

I flung hair out of my face and peered up at the boat. One of the females was driving, of course. Men were forbidden to drive any of the resort's boats, and for good reason: My sisters loved to siren call any young man who got close to our island, smile and beckon to him, then send a whirlpool or wave to crash his boat or canoe against the rocks. They never harmed anyone, yet such activities were generally frowned upon. By the human women, anyway. Mother once told us that some humans talked about banning us, but everyone knew that the sirens at Faraway Lake attracted new young men to the resort every summer. Even though few of them ever caught a glimpse of us, there was always a chance.

The boat drew near, and a large hand appeared in front of me. It had soft skin, like my hands, but there was black hair growing on the arm above it. How hideous! Why did male and female humans both have soft hands? A man should have webbed hands and feet, and scales on his arms and face. My sister Moselle often wondered aloud how humans tell the males from the females, and the rest of us always nodded in agreement.

But now that I looked at a human male up close, he was obviously not female. He wore no clothing on his top half, and only short trousers on his bottom half. That much seemed familiar: Mermen wear trousers and their chests are bare. But this human male's chest and belly were hairy—not thick fur like a beaver's, but it still creeped me out. I allowed him to grasp my arm and haul me up into the boat in one swift movement. He was strong, as a man should be, and his muscles were well defined. As a siren I shouldn't have noticed this, but I couldn't really help it.

I turned away and looked at the females. "Thank you," I panted. Not until I saw their garments did it occur to me to wonder what I was wearing. I glanced down to see, with a tremendous

3

sense of relief, that I wore not only my usual traditional wrap-top decorated with paua-shell chips, but also a short pair of trousers of the same seaweed-filament fabric.

Now that I was out of the water, wind blew on my skin and chilled me further. My clothing clung to my skin, and strange bumps rose on my arms. As a siren I had never felt the cold, but I seemed to have lost that power along with my tail. "I'm freezing!" I said, and my chin quivered as I spoke.

"Here, take my towel." A young female who wore her black hair in a long braid wrapped me in a thick cloth and pushed me into a seat in the back of the boat. "How did you get out in the middle of the bay all by yourself? Were you trying to swim across the lake?"

I shrugged and nodded. That seemed as good a reason as any.

"Don't talk nonsense, Eddi," said the other female, who appeared to be around my age. She looked at me with perceptive eyes and smiled. "You're a siren, aren't you? Or rather, you were. And now you're human. How exciting!"

The younger girl's mouth dropped open. "A siren? Like, a real mermaid?" Her bright eyes looked me up and down. "You're right. She's too gorgeous to be human." She gave the young man a pointed look. "Like you, Mike."

He stood looking down at us, feet braced as the boat rocked, arms crossed over his broad chest. "I am not too gorgeous to be human, Eddi. I am simply the handsomest human you've ever seen." He flashed her a smile. "You enjoyed watching me waterski."

Eddi blinked dreamy eyes. "You were rather amazing to watch."

Human girls found this sort of man attractive? I had never been more thankful to not be human. But wait. I was human. *Oh dear.*

"My name is Beatrice. What's yours?" the older girl asked as she sat sideways in the driver's seat, still facing me.

"Kamoana."

"What a pretty name!" She looked intrigued. "I've heard stories about merfolk taking human form, but I never in my life imagined I might meet one!"

When I coughed and sneezed (another new experience that startled me), Beatrice's smooth brow wrinkled. "Here I am, waiting to hear your life story while you might need to see a doctor. Sit down, you two."

Eddi sat beside me, and the man, Mike, dropped into another seat as Beatrice started the boat moving. His chair spun around until he faced me, and I felt his stare like a concentrated beam of sunlight, burning and uncomfortable. Foam and spray dashed up on either side of the boat as it accelerated.

"You were coughing awfully hard. We thought you were drowning at first," Eddi told me, shouting above the noise of engine, wind, and waves. "I'm Princess Edurne of Bilbao, but everyone calls me Eddi, so please do. Beatrice is my companion."

"Companion?"

"A fancy name for a maid," Beatrice called back over her shoulder. She must have excellent hearing, I thought.

"More like a big sister," Eddi amended. "She tries to keep me out of trouble. So, will you ever tell us why you're here? I mean, as a human?"

"Maybe," I said, glancing from Eddi to Beatrice to the man. In truth, what little I could recall was fuzzy. But I did know one thing for certain: "I really need to see the resort director."

"We can take you to her," Beatrice said, then called back over her shoulder, "Your Highness, do you wish to be introduced to Kamoana?"

The man they called Mike had been observing me all this time, his elbows on his knees with those fleshy hands hanging down between. His eyes were the color of amber. Very pretty, I had to admit. He had thick black eyelashes any girl would envy and thick black brows no girl would want. His chin was dark, as if hair tried to grow there too. Even his legs were hairy. Were all human men that hairy? I tried to hide a shudder.

Mike smiled as if he knew what I was thinking. Or, more likely, he thought I liked the way he looked. He was certainly quite pleased with himself. "I'll introduce myself," he answered Beatrice, his gaze never leaving my face. "I am Prince Michael of Dorintosh, a fabulous kingdom on the other side of the world in the Far North. I'm enjoying the sunshine and heat here."

"That's nice." I tried not to look at him again.

We roared across the lake so fast that I felt as if I might fly out of the boat at any second. Wind whipped at my hair until it wrapped around my face. I clutched at the towel around my shoulders and hoped to live through the next few minutes. Surely the director of Faraway Castle Resort would be able to contact Mother and get me back to where I belonged. Back into my proper shape. I could hardly look down for the horror of seeing those legs where my tail should be.

Princess Eddi leaned forward to ask, "Are you going to be human for good?"

My eyes widened. "I certainly hope not."

"How did you get turned human?"

"I'm . . . not sure. Magic, of course, but I don't remember why."

"Or *who*," Eddi added, nodding sagely. "You've lost your memory. I bet there is some man you need to find and fall in love with to break the spell. That's how these things usually work."

"A human man?" I must have sounded horrified, because Eddi laughed.

"You don't like human men? What about Mike?" She waved a hand toward the man lounging on his seat, his limbs splayed out, his head tipped back. He now wore dark glasses over his eyes. Merfolk don't have vision problems, so I wondered how I knew the device was called "glasses," but it didn't seem to matter just then. More important questions existed.

"I'm sure he is an excellent person," I said. "But I don't know him at all."

He lifted the glasses and smiled at me, raising one brow. "We can solve that problem easily enough, Kamoana. Want me to come and sit beside you?"

I sat further into my corner. "No, thank you."

Eddi looked at me as if I were crazy. Beatrice appeared to focus on driving the boat, but even from behind I thought she might be laughing. "Kamoana," she called over her shoulder. "Will you need help walking?"

"I don't know," I admitted. "I've never tried to do it before."

Mike laughed at this and sat upright again.

"What is so funny about that?" I asked.

Instead of answering, he said, "You are a gorgeous woman, Kamoana. But then, all sirens are gorgeous."

Eddi gazed at him in wonder. "Have you seen a siren, Prince Mike?"

"I have. She spoke to me." One dark brow twitched again. "Even sirens find me irresistible. But a human-siren match could never work out. I let her down gently."

Oh, gag me. If all humans were this inane, my time as a woman would be fraught with horror. I needed to find the director and get put back to normal, and fast!

2

BEATRICE STEERED THE boat directly toward the docks, which seemed to rush toward us. A beach crawling with humans lay beyond the docks, and beyond the beach a path led through the trees and up to Faraway Castle. This view was familiar, though the angle was new. I had spent most of my life within sight of that beautiful castle. Very soon, for the first time, I was to enter it.

Beatrice eased the boat into an open space, and I watched with interest as she and Eddi hopped out and tied ropes to metal brackets on the dock. One of the resort staff members came to help secure the boat—she kept smiling at Mike while he sat in the boat and watched the girls work. "Good job, ladies," he called.

"Thank you, Mike." Eddi gave him an eager smile. She was still very young. Hopefully she would learn to have better taste, given time.

Beatrice caught my eye and winked. Good to know that not all human women admired hairy egotists. Prince Michael hopped onto the dock and held out a hand to assist me. I didn't want to need his help, but I did. As soon as my feet hit the dock, I would have fallen if not for his supporting hand under my arm.

"What's wrong?" Eddi asked. "Are you all right?"

I looked down at my feet, quickly closed my eyes, then peered at them again between my lashes. "It feels so weird! How do you ever balance?"

Mermen had legs and feet, of course, but theirs were green or silvery and slimy, not tan with pink toenails. And their feet had webbing between the toes.

"You'll get used to it," Mike said. "Feet aren't so bad."

"Easy for you to say. You've never had a tail!" I retorted, trying to sound amused.

"Before long you'll be running around like the rest of us!" Eddi assured me from Mike's other side.

"Thank you, but I'm hoping to not be human that long," I said firmly. Hearing a little gasp, I looked up to see the lifeguard girl staring at me with open mouth. No use trying to explain—I simply needed to get back to my proper form, and fast. I turned to Beatrice, the most practical human I'd met thus far. "May I see the resort director now?"

Her eyes glinted with amusement. "Let's head to the castle. Follow me. I'm sure we'll find the director in her office or nearby."

"I never did get to water ski," Eddi sighed as she started after her friend. "You must try skiing while you're human, Kamoana. It's super fun. Kind of like flying."

"More like swimming very fast," said Mike, still supporting my forearm, "but with wind in your face as you slide across the surface."

Over one shoulder, Eddi gave him a raised-eyebrow look. "Flying," she repeated.

Ha! Maybe she was starting to catch on? She trotted ahead to catch up with Beatrice, leaving me alone with Mike, who was exchanging smiles with the blonde lifeguard. "I'm Kerry Jo, and I work at the lake every day," the girl said breathlessly.

"Good to know," said Mike, his tone caressing. The girl fluttered like a jellyfish.

Enough of this. I tottered away on unsteady legs, and Mike walked beside me with that supporting hand still under my elbow. When I tried to pull away, his hand simply followed my arm as if it had stuck there. When I glared at him, he smiled into my eyes, his expression downright gooey.

Uh oh. Was he siren-enthralled? But he couldn't be! I hadn't done anything to attract him. Nothing deliberate, anyway. I tried to walk faster but tripped and had to catch hold of his other hand to keep from falling on my face. For all I didn't want his help, I didn't know how to use these stupid legs. When we stepped off the end of the dock, the hot sand burned my tender feet. I sort of hopped along until we reached a stretch where grass grew.

Beatrice and Eddi turned in time to see me wince and shift my weight from foot to foot while Mike held my arm and grinned. "Kamoana, I'm so sorry!" Beatrice said and hurried back to us. "Here, you can wear these." She pulled off her shoes.

They were sparkly flat things with straps that went between my toes. Awkward, but they kept my feet off the ground, and the flat part was cushiony. I took a few trial steps and sighed in relief. "Thank you."

"They fit you," Eddi said. "First shoes you've ever worn!"

"Hush," said Beatrice. "Better not to advertise."

It was then I realized that people were staring. I felt as if every human on the beach watched us. No doubt that perception was exaggerated, but my embarrassment was real. I suddenly wished for an anti-siren charm that would drive human men away. Particularly the one holding my arm.

Beatrice and Eddi wore long, dry wraps to cover their bodies. I had only my chest wrap, short trousers that clung to my new legs like a second skin, and a towel around my shoulders. "I need more clothes," I said.

"Again, I'm not thinking straight. Here you go." Beatrice wrapped a second towel around my waist. "Tuck it in, like this, and wear it like a sarong. I'm sorry I didn't think to offer it sooner."

"Thank you." The staring didn't stop, but at least there was less of me in view. Strange . . . I'd never felt self-conscious as a siren. Modesty couldn't be just a human thing, because Mike displayed his muscular body like a male betta fish showing off its colorful fins. Again, I attempted to free my arm, but I might as well have tried to escape a barnacle.

The girls led the way along the tree-lined path to the castle, quietly talking together. Doing my best to ignore Mike, I enjoyed viewing the castle itself, glimpses of its gardens, and the mountains that surrounded us. Of course, I had seen this view from every possible spot in the lake, but never before had I ventured onto land. Well, except for a few rocks on the lake's perimeter. And maybe once or twice I had scooted up a beach a short way. Never when humans were around to see me, of course. I'd had that much sense even as a young girl.

Or had I?

As soon as doubt entered my mind, a memory popped up with it: I sat on a familiar rock near the shore west of the castle, and someone sat on a ledge above me, his legs dangling into the water at my side. Skinny, hairy legs. A human male. Yet I was eating a piece of fruit and feeling intensely happy.

Shocked, I forgot to pick my feet up and tripped over the shoes. Mike squeezed my elbow. "You're doing well, Kamoana. Just a little farther, and we'll be at the castle. See the doors straight ahead?"

I gave him a look. "Your Highness, I may be a siren, but I do have a brain, and I know where the castle is."

My best icy tone simply melted and dripped off his hotness. "But you've never been inside a building before," he said, gently shaking my arm, "so you don't know how doors work."

"I think I can figure it out," I growled, tugging at my elbow. The barnacle held fast.

Faraway Castle was more of a handsome manor, once owned by a wealthy human. Mother had told me the story, but I seldom paid attention and was hazy on the details. It was common knowledge that the owner had allowed his property to be turned into a resort for royals, nobles, and wealthy people from all over the world, who found it a safe place to escape from staring, clutching, critical crowds for a time and to associate with people of their own class and rank.

What a relief it must be to feel normal, even ordinary, for a short time while among people of equal rank in the world! I never felt normal anywhere.

The resort staff consisted mainly of young humans of ordinary social status, all having some inherent magical ability. People of higher social and economic status who possessed magical talent were sent to schools for the magically gifted, but common people could not afford the tuition. Faraway Castle offered its staff members a place to associate with other people of similar abilities and the opportunity to legally practice and develop their magical gifts. Again, a place to fit in.

The resort grounds were also a sort of refuge for many magical beings. Including my family, although my mother had moved our tropical-island home here to this lake high in the mountains of Adelboden before I was born. Many brownies, dwarfs, and other magical beings lived and worked in or near the castle, where they were safe and productive. Others, such as pixies, cinder sprites, and sirens, were useless when it came to work but added to the magical ambiance . . . or so we told ourselves.

Being exotic and decorative satisfied my sisters. Me? Not so much.

And then there was Nelumbo, the lake monster. He got his kicks by frightening humans, but he never harmed anyone. Much. Nelumbo and I had shared many adventures . . .

I stopped there on the path and stared toward the sparkling lake. I couldn't recollect many of those adventures. Why not? A sense of loss filled that strange void in my memories, my head suddenly ached, and my own magic flared up, bringing a burst of sensory—

"Kamoana?" Beatrice said, startling me out of my trance. "We're here." She and Eddi stood directly in front of me, looking concerned. "Are you all right?"

I had stopped just outside the portico at the castle's entrance. Mike, who still held my arm, gazed down at me with such patronizing amusement that I immediately recovered my senses.

"Oh," I said. "I'm sorry. I was . . . trying to remember something."

I tucked the weird memory away for later contemplation. I wasn't generally susceptible to intense emotions such as delight or despair. Turning away from my lake, I deliberately focused on the glass doors. People swarmed in and out of the great building, mostly in chattering, happy groups. I saw humans in swimwear, in short trousers and tee shirts, and in clothing that covered all except their heads and hands. The women wore their hair in all manner of styles, from long and loose like mine to quite short. All were well dressed and elegant in their manner.

Except those who turned to stare. Then they were rude. The women's chilly glances skimmed over me, fastened on Mike still resplendent in his hairy skin, and melted into syrupy pools. A few of them called to him, "Prince Mike! Sit with me at dinner?" or "Your Highness, want to go boating?" He waved, showed numerous white teeth in that irritating smile, and replied that he was busy just now.

They looked crushed by his refusal and gave me daggered stares. As if I wanted him! He did open the door for me, which was considerate, since I wasn't sure how and didn't want anyone to guess. "This way," Beatrice said with a little wave.

We crossed a large room with a domed ceiling made largely of colored glass. The light falling through it splashed the room with blue and gold and reminded me of being underwater in a tropical lagoon. Humans were everywhere. A dwarf wearing a glamour that made him look human stood behind a desk. Dozens of brownies scuttled here and there. My mother had raised me to be polite to brownies, so I smiled at a few nearby. Some of them smiled back; others stared at me in awe. Perhaps they recognized me as my mother's daughter. There was some power in being well connected.

Eddi spun toward Beatrice. "I just saw Kai get in the elevator, and I've got to talk to him about the group ride Sunday. I'll be back in a minute." Without waiting for an answer, she dashed off, and I saw her enter a tiny room just before the door closed.

Beatrice turned to me with concern in her eyes, and I latched hold of her wrist. "Come with me?" I begged.

"Of course. Princess Edurne will know how to find us." Her brow knitted. "Are you sure you want us there?"

At my definite nod, Beatrice paused at a door in a wall and rapped on it with her knuckles. A muffled voice called, "Enter." Beatrice led the way, and I came next, with Mike still dangling from my elbow like a tenacious piece of seaweed. I didn't want him along, but it wasn't worth a public battle.

Madame Genevieve, the director of Faraway Castle Resort, sat in a chair, her posture straight, her hands folded on a large desk. She surveyed me, from my messy hair down to those sparkly shoes, in one sweeping glance. "Kamoana, your mother told me you would be coming today." Then her eyes rested on Mike and softened into sunlit pools of green. "Ah, Your Highness, I trust your stay at Faraway Castle is going well?"

At last he released my arm, stepping forward to take her hand. "Couldn't be better," he said with drippy cheerfulness and cast me an eloquent look. "I found a beautiful siren, you see."

3

I CHOKED BUT TURNED it into a cough. Mike sounded as if I'd siren-charmed him. If I'd known how to kick him in the shin, I might have resorted to violence. But it wouldn't have done any good—he probably would view a swift kick as flirtation.

The director glanced at my other companion. "Miss de Callen." Her tone was distant yet cordial. Beatrice murmured a polite greeting as Madame's attention returned to me. "I expected a private meeting."

"Madame Genevieve," I said, "these two found me while I was transforming, so they already know my secret." I didn't want to be left alone with her. Even Mike's presence was some protection. When I was a child, the resort director had frequently dropped in at our island without notice. She was on first-name basis with my mother, the only human I knew of with that privilege. Back then she seemed to like me well enough, but sometime during my teens her tolerance had turned to spite. She was a tall woman with golden-brown skin, thick dark hair, and those stunning green eyes . . . To be honest, she was quite beautiful except for her stony expression, with only a few fine lines around her set mouth to reveal her age.

"Very well, if that is your choice. What do you expect me to explain?" she asked, her long fingers tapping the backs of her folded hands. "What do you know?"

"I know only that Mother told me to come to you first thing, and you would tell me what to do. I don't even know why I'm in"—I looked down at my legs—"human form." Remembering Eddi's guess, I asked, "Is this some kind of test?" I must have angered Mother somehow. This couldn't be about romance; I'd never been seriously interested in anyone . . . not that I could recall.

Madame almost smiled—her scariest expression yet. "So Pukai really did strip your memories. It was only fair, considering your many advantages." She seemed to be talking more to herself than to me, but then she leaned slightly forward and gave me a decided nod. "Very well, I'll tell you. Yes, this is a test, a three-day love test. Your mother turned you human because for—what is it now?—six or seven years, at least, you've declared yourself in love with a human boy, and you have more than once defied her authority by meeting with him in secret."

I distinctly heard Beatrice gasp. My heart seemed to thunder in my chest. "No! That's ridiculous!" My voice squeaked.

Behind me, I thought I heard Mike stifle a laugh and Beatrice hushing him. Why, oh why had I brought human strangers into the office with me?

"I couldn't . . . I couldn't possibly be in love with a human," I stammered. "Mother must have misunderstood. Maybe she saw me speak with a human about my studies?" I had no memory of speaking with any human about any such thing, but this supposition seemed more plausible than romance. After all, someone had supplied me with scientific textbooks and journals to read. "Maybe Mother mistook my love of knowledge for love of a teacher, or something like that. You know very well that I've never wanted to marry. I refuse to give up my dream of getting a degree in ocean science."

"Indeed?" A cruel sort of humor glowed in her eyes. "Only yesterday I stood beside your mother while you declared yourself ready to give up anything to be with this human."

Mike mumbled something, and again Beatrice hushed him.

My legs trembled beneath me. Fearing they would give out altogether, I gripped the edge of her desk. "I don't believe it. Who? Show him to me."

Madame ignored my bluster. "Queen Pukai finally had enough. She decided to take you at your word and teach you a good lesson."

"By turning me into a human?" I pointed at my toes. "How can this teach me anything? Where is this human I liked so much?"

"I would imagine he is nearby." Her gaze flickered toward Mike. "But his identity is for you to discover. If he is as right for you as you seemed to believe, surely you can find him and make him love you again within three days. Naturally, your mother removed his memories of you as well."

"Naturally," I echoed grimly, "she wouldn't make passing this test actually possible."

Madame continued as if I hadn't spoken. "Your mother has supplied you with everything you need to pass yourself off as a wealthy human while you're at the resort. You are supposedly my visiting niece, a girl of good family from Singkiang, a human country near your ancestral home."

"I know where it is," I snapped. "Do I have human clothing to wear? I can't walk around in my wrap and merman trousers all the time!"

"True, your present attire is scandalous. You are to sleep in room three fourteen, and all clothing and possessions you need are waiting there for you. Here is the key." She handed me a strangely shaped piece of metal.

"What is this for?"

"It will enable you to open the door."

I stared at the key. "If you say so."

"We'll show you how to do it, Kamoana," Mike said, and stepped forward to hug my shoulders. I nearly yelped. His arm was bare and warm where it touched my skin, and he pulled me close to his side, which was even worse. If I was inappropriately dressed, then so was he!

I looked to Beatrice for help, and the girl came through for me. "Tell you what, I'll run up to my room and bring you a wrap, so you don't have to walk through the lobby again wearing wet clothes and towels. I'll be right back." And she slipped out the door.

As soon as she was gone, I ducked out of Mike's grasp—leaving my towel in his hand—then stepped close to the director's desk and propped my hands on its surface. "I need more information. Please tell me when I knew this human. Did I meet him recently?"

She raised a satirical brow. "Think back over what I have already said, and you will find your answer." She lowered her gaze and picked up a stack of papers. "I have work to do. Go and seek your adventure." Her voice held neither warmth nor goodwill, but that was nothing new.

I reclaimed my towel and hurried out of her office with Mike close behind. I felt steadier on my feet already. My legs felt less foreign, though I still tripped over my toes occasionally. But everything ached, even my back. Walking used my muscles and bones in all new ways.

People still stared at me, and now I knew that my lack of clothing was at fault. My face felt strangely warm, and I clutched the towels closer. I glanced at Mike. He was showing a lot more skin than I was. "Don't you need to put more clothes on too? No other human here is wearing only short trousers."

He looked down at himself. "These are swim trunks, and what does it matter? I'm comfortable, and women like looking at me."

"I don't."

He gave me a knowing smile. "Yes, you do. You just don't want to admit how much you enjoy it."

What was the point in arguing with someone that blind to reality? Though he did have a point about the women. As we stood there near a wall in the lobby, waiting for Beatrice to return, several young women cast glances Mike's way and giggled. Some greeted him by name. Others merely looked him up and down and fluttered their eyes. This alone was reason to avoid being in his presence. It was truly horrifying.

Not that I hadn't seen much the same behavior from my fellow sirens when they admired a merman. I couldn't think of his name, but there'd been one guy my sisters admired possibly even more than their husbands. Some prince or lord.

This time both Beatrice and Eddi appeared in that mysterious doorway and walked out of the tiny room. Three other people entered the room as they walked out, and the doors closed again. I realized it must be some kind of portal like our water doors.

While Eddi engaged Mike in conversation, Beatrice pulled me into a side room with "Women" printed on the door and held out a pink-flowered garment. "Here you go."

I dropped the towels and slipped my arms through the holes she indicated, then tied long strands of fabric around my waist as she directed, relieved to be mostly hidden from curious eyes. I didn't care so much about people seeing my upper half, which hadn't changed at all, but a girl's lower half should be modestly covered with pretty scales, not bare skin.

I had sense enough to keep this opinion to myself. "Thank you, Beatrice," I said sincerely. "I don't know what I would have done if you hadn't shown up today!"

She patted my shoulder in a sisterly way as we returned to the lobby. "You're smart and tough, and you would have figured things out. You can thank Mike for wanting to waterski in that particular area of the lake."

Mike caught my eye and wriggled his brows. I quickly looked away.

"He skied so long that I didn't get a chance," Eddi reminded us. "But it was exciting to find a real mermaid and bring her back with us. Beatrice wouldn't tell me what happened in the director's office. Did you find out how to break the spell, Kamoana?"

"She has to find the human she's in love with," Mike answered before I could open my mouth.

"I can't imagine being in love with a human." I glared up at his smirking face.

"What's the big difference between male humans and mermen?" Eddi asked.

Just then two young women walked up to Mike, and one said, "We've dared each other to introduce ourselves to you. I'm

Raquel and this is Gillian, and we both think you're the most gorgeous man we've ever seen."

"How I admire beautiful and perceptive women!" Mike flashed his smile and flexed a few muscles here and there.

I grabbed Beatrice and Eddi each by an arm and hustled them away. "I cannot bear being around him another moment. I hope he's not a close friend of yours. But even if he is, I can't endure him."

Beatrice laughed aloud. Eddi, looking puzzled, said, "We don't really know him; I think he just arrived at the resort a day or so ago. But he truly must be the handsomest man ever, and he's an amazing skier, and he's super strong. And he always smiles. I've never seen him frown. He's the one who spotted you struggling in the water, so you do owe him a little."

"Maybe so, but I believe I've thanked him enough. Are all human men that egotistical?"

Beatrice shook her head, but Eddi answered first, "Most of the guys here are rich and titled, and quite a few are handsome, so I guess most of them are about as vain as Mike."

I was tempted to take a boat out to the island, find Mother, and give her a piece of my mind. This was the most ridiculous escapade she'd ever started. At least, as far as I could remember. Which wasn't far.

Beatrice, still chuckling, took charge and led us to that portal room. When the doors opened, I followed her and Eddi inside. I sensed no magic at all, yet when the doors shut themselves, I felt the room begin to rise. After a brief panic, I realized this was how humans moved from lower levels to higher places in the castle, since they couldn't float in air the way we floated in water. As a child I had wondered about that. Funny, how children often notice things adults pass over.

"Kamoana, are you all right?" asked Beatrice.

"Yes!" I blurted, then loosened my death-grip on the rail surrounding the room. "I mean, yes, I'm fine. I've never been in a moving room before."

"It's called an elevator, since it elevates us," Eddi said. "The ones here are awfully slow and break down a lot, but they're better than stairs. I guess you wouldn't need them underwater. I never thought of that before! So, you've never been on land, right?"

"Not that I recall, and I wouldn't think I'd forget something like that. I mean, I've sat on rocks in the lake, and maybe scooted up on shore a little now and then." Remembering my earlier flash of memory, I frowned. That particular rock was a secret perch of mine. Had I really shared it with a human boy and eaten his food? I must have. Mother could block memories, but she couldn't add or edit them, and she certainly couldn't simulate the joy I'd experienced during that flash of memory.

"How do you think you met this human you love?" Eddi persisted.

I slowly shook my head. "I have no idea. I'm not allowed to speak to humans, and I can't imagine why or how I would have broken that rule."

Yet, beyond doubt, I had broken it. And felt blissfully happy while doing so.

"But if you met a handsome human guy, maybe you couldn't help yourself."

Automatically I responded, "That could never happen. Sirens don't find human men attractive."

Except for my fleeting thoughts about Mike on the boat—I had noticed his striking eyes and strong muscles. My sisters would have fits if they knew. Maybe being turned human had altered my perceptions?

Eddi asked, "Then why did—"

"I don't know; I don't remember," I snapped.

My rudeness had no effect on Princess Edurne. "Mike is so gorgeous he hardly seems real, yet you don't seem to like him at all," she observed.

"His appearance isn't the problem," I said, realizing it as truth, and I saw Beatrice stifle another laugh.

"Well, we know you find at least one human male attractive." Beatrice voiced the truth I was trying to ignore: "So attractive that your mother turned you human so you could find him."

Just then the elevator doors opened, and we were in a different place.

4

A LONG HALLWAY LAY before us, with doors on each side. My aching feet and legs would have groaned if they could. Walking was hard work!

"Your room should be down here on the left." Beatrice led the way. We stopped before a door with the numeral 314 on it, and I handed over the key and observed how she used it.

As the door swung open, Eddi cried, "Welcome to your room in Faraway Castle," and ran into a spacious room with tall windows offering a stunning panorama of Faraway Lake. At first glance the view was idyllic, with Palau Kalah, my family's island, like a green jewel against sparkling blue. But if I squinted and tilted my head, the island was too large to fit into that corner of Faraway Lake.

I gave my head a shake and opened my eyes wide. Once again, the view was tranquil, the lake clear and blue, dotted with sailboats and ski boats. Snow-topped mountains ringed the resort like silvery sentinels, but Mt. Ibu, the little volcano at

Palau Kalah's northwest end, puffed smoke. It did that whenever Mother was in a temper.

"Come and look in your washroom," Eddi ordered, beckoning. "It will be all new to you!"

The girls showed me how to turn the water faucets on and off, and how to flush the toilet. I did find it all rather fascinating. The looking glass over the wash basin startled me. My face and upper body hadn't changed, and my hair was as long and glossy as ever, though rather messy. But from the waist down . . . My legs gave me a start every time I glimpsed them, though they functioned well when I didn't forget to put one foot in front of the other. I missed my lovely iridescent tail.

If I passed my mother's test, if I found the right human man and he loved me again and asked to marry me, would I lose my tail forever? And my island home? My siren magic? How could anyone be worth that much sacrifice? What if he loved me and broke the spell and I stayed human . . . but later changed my mind? What if the man I thought I loved turned out to be a tyrant or a jerk? What if he wouldn't allow me to pursue my education?

I stared at my reflection in the glass while terror froze me to the bone. Only an idiot would try to break this spell! I should just have fun for three days and learn all I could about the human world, then get my tail and my life back and tell my mother she was right.

And yet . . . at some time very recently, I had believed him worth the sacrifice. The memories of *why* I believed this were gone. Did I trust myself enough to rush ahead and try to break this spell while I remembered none of my reasons for doing so?

Once more my vision blurred, and a strange feeling touched my heart and spirit, a yearning for something I didn't understand. A memory of love? My hands lifted to press over my heart.

My magic was nothing compared to my mother's, yet memories seemed to be leaking through her spell. If I concentrated hard, could I bring back more of them? And if I identified my human, might I help him remember me?

"Kamoana, may we help you unpack?" Beatrice asked from the other room.

Lost in thoughts and fears, I hadn't even noticed when she and Eddi left. I joined them in the main room. "Please do."

"Beatrice is great at organizing a wardrobe," Eddi informed me, already pulling garments from a boxy object on the floor, while Beatrice unpacked another. "I can hang up stuff."

I figured out how to open another one of the four "travel bags," as Eddi called them, and within minutes we had garments strewn about the room. "I'm not sure what to do with some of these things," I admitted. The various shirts, trousers, and swimsuits were self-explanatory, and even my mother wore dresses when she assumed human form. But the pieces of silky fabric and fluff?

Stifling giggles, my new friends explained the practicality of undergarments and nightwear, even those made mostly of lace and ribbon. Beatrice soon sent me into the washroom with clothing to put on—including white skinny jeans and a ruffled coral-pink top. I brushed out my hair as Eddi had shown me and tied it back with a matching pink ribbon. There were comfortable white shoes called "sneakers" for my feet. My mother must have supplied this wardrobe, and judging by my new friends' reactions, she had excellent taste.

It was when I picked up my discarded wrap top that a gold ring on a chain dropped to the floor. I lifted the chain to examine the beautifully engraved gold band, just the right size to slide on my finger. Inside my garment I found a tiny pocket of a different fabric, exactly large enough to hold the jewelry. The sewing looked like my handiwork, so I must not have wanted anyone to know about the chain and ring. I considered fastening it around my neck now but ended up tucking it into a drawer.

The girls looked delighted when I returned to model my new look. "Perfect!" Beatrice declared. "We've stowed your clothing in this wardrobe and this chest of drawers. You have some beautiful things! This gown will be perfect for the Summer Ball this Saturday," she said, holding up a shimmery mass of blue fabric. I thought with a pang that it looked like my tail.

"The Summer Ball?"

"The biggest event of the season," Beatrice explained. "Do you know how to dance?"

"Not on feet."

Eddi laughed and gave Beatrice a look. "We could teach her to dance," she said as if requesting a favor. Beatrice nodded approval, and Eddi beamed. "Dancing lessons. Yes!"

"But first, lunch." Beatrice beckoned me to the vanity. "Don't forget that your toiletries are in this drawer," she said, tapping its front. "And your shampoo and conditioner are in the shower."

"What are they for?"

Both girls paused as if to gather their thoughts, then Beatrice explained, "They're for cleaning your hair while you shower. You can read the directions printed on the bottles. Be sure to use the shampoo first, then the conditioner. It will help keep your hair soft and healthy."

This made sense. "Yes, I suppose my hair will dry out while I'm not in the water. Is there something to keep my skin from drying out as well?"

Beatrice showed me hand and body lotions, toothbrush and toothpaste, and explained the use of each. "Do I seem very strange to you?" I asked during a pause.

Eddi perched on a chair and looked uncomfortable. But Beatrice smiled at me. "You are not strange, but human ways are strange and new to you. We would feel just as confused in your world. Now, we'd better head downstairs and help you find Mr. Right."

"Is that his name?" I asked without thinking first.

This time, both Eddi and Beatrice burst out laughing. After a blushing moment, I joined them. "You meant that you want to help find the right man for me. I get it," I said once they quieted. "I hope I don't make a complete fool of myself in the next few days."

"You'll be fine," Beatrice assured me. "People from many countries and continents mingle together here, so communication mix-ups happen all the time."

As we gathered my room key and our little handbags, I said, "Thank you for all this help." Mere thanks seemed inadequate. "I think now I can figure out what to wear, and even which shoes."

"If you mess up, we'll tell you," Eddi offered cheerily.

As we left the room, Beatrice showed me how to lock the door and made certain I placed my room key into my tiny purse, saying, "Be sure to keep track of your handbag." I listened carefully to her directions about how to find my room again but feared I would forget everything I was supposed to know.

"It's time for lunch, so we'll head down to the dining hall."
Beatrice led the way again. "I think we should try the stairs this
time. You'll need to get used to them."

"Sure!" My new shoes and clothing built up my confidence.
"I'm ready to conquer the human world."

Or so I thought until we entered the stairwell. The sight of
that jagged cliff descending so quickly gave me the judders.

"Hold on to the banister and take one step at a time. It's
not as difficult as it looks," Eddi said, sounding like a big sister.

When I reached the first landing, both girls praised me. "I
feel so clumsy and strange," I said. "I'm just not sure I can handle
pretending to be human. Everyone will know I'm a fake."

"They won't," Beatrice said. "They're too worried about
themselves to notice."

"I can't believe I'm hanging out with a siren! No one would
believe it," Eddi gushed, then gave me an evaluating look. "How
old are you?"

"Twenty-two." Clutching the rail with both hands, I started
down the next cliffside, stepping down with my left foot first
each time.

"No way! Really? You're the same age as Beatrice. I thought
you were closer to my age," Eddi said. "I'm sixteen."

Sixteen. The age I was when . . . When I lost something
important. I blinked, again sensing the brief snap of magic.

My legs and hands were shaking by the time we stepped
from the stairwell into the lobby, but I enjoyed a sense of
accomplishment. "This way," Beatrice said, and we headed toward
a set of doors. Few guests were in the lobby at mealtime. Brownies
swarmed across the floor, and this time several of them returned
my smile. The dwarf at the front desk also gave me a wave.

A long window composed one entire wall of the dining hall, offering another perfect view of Faraway Lake. A relief. Until today I had never been out of sight and touch of water.

We sat at a small table with places for four. The meal amazed me. Brownies brought plates to our table, but neither Beatrice nor Eddi seemed able to see the little creatures. "How do the plates get to the table?" I asked them, examining my meal with suspicion.

"Magic, of course," Eddi said with a grin. "This is Faraway Castle, after all. You're a siren. Can't you detect magic?"

"Oh yes," I answered. "I just wondered if you could."

"We can't detect it at all, Kamoana," Beatrice said in her serene way as she unfolded a white cloth and laid it over her lap. "I imagine you see a great deal more in this room than we do. To us, the plates simply appear before us when we sit down."

"Oh." I followed her example, spreading an identical cloth on my own lap.

I met the gaze of a brownie at my elbow, who smiled and said, "Be sure to eat the brown square thing. We all like them best," in a high-pitched little voice.

I nodded.

"Don't do that!" Eddi paused with a forkful of food halfway to her mouth. "Don't nod like that, I mean. It kind of freaks me out. Some of the other guests say they can see little people, but I'd rather not think about something I can't see."

"All right." I found her attitude puzzling.

Then Eddi looked past me, and her face brightened.

"Here you are!" A deep, hearty voice gave my stomach a jolt.

5

P RINCE MIKE!" EDDI dropped her fork and beamed up at him. "We've got another chair for you." She indicated the empty chair beside mine.

I didn't look around until he was seated. He was fully clothed, which was a pleasant surprise, and he smelled nice. His elbow bumped mine as he spread a cloth over his lap. Feeling uneasy, I glanced up to find Mike staring at me with evident satisfaction. "You're catching on fast," he commented. "And you look great."

"Thank you." His attention only increased my discomfort. I looked away and noticed how many people at other tables were watching us.

A brownie slid a plate onto the table before Mike. "Hmm. Swordfish." He picked up a piece of green food with his fingers and popped it into his mouth. "Eat up, ladies," he said, still chewing.

I glanced at my friends, who pointedly focused on their own meals. Watching how they used the silver utensils on the table, I copied their movements and managed to get most of the food neatly into my mouth. I was rather slow at it, but no one seemed to mind. The sweet pink drink was easy enough to handle, and I enjoyed its taste.

Best of all was that brown square recommended to me by the brownie. "Oh," I cried after the first chewy bite. "What is this? It's amazing!"

"It's a brownie," Eddi said, sounding pleased.

No doubt my face reflected the surge of horror I experienced at her answer, because Mike burst into laughter. "Not that kind of brownie," he said, and his voice seemed to carry across the room. Again we were the focus of far too many stares.

"It's a baked treat made with chocolate," Beatrice told me in her quiet way. "Maybe the treats were named for the little magical creatures? Who knows."

"Brownies are my favorite." Eddi took a huge bite of hers. "I could eat them all day long."

"So could I," Mike said.

I watched as another brownie slid a plate full of the brown squares onto the table. The little creature winked at me and rushed away.

"Look, more brownies!" Eddi exclaimed. "Did you do that, Kamoana?"

"No, they must have heard us talking," I said. "Brownies—the people, that is—love to please. Mother always told me they live to work and serve other people. They must be the most unselfish beings alive."

Mike shrugged. "Whatever. So long as we get fed. The swordfish steak was overcooked, and I don't care for that soggy orange stuff."

"It is a casserole," Beatrice explained, "made from sweet potatoes."

"Whatever." He picked up the last chunk of fish and shoved it into his mouth. Liquid dripped on the front of his shirt. "Eh," he grumbled, brushing at it.

"Use your serviette," Beatrice said, indicating the cloth in her own lap.

Mike scrubbed at the spot with his serviette, but it wouldn't fade. "I'm not at my best today." He glanced over at me. "Even so, no man in the room is my equal."

"And we're all thankful for these small blessings," I said sweetly. Beatrice covered her mouth with her serviette, and her shoulders shook.

Mike beamed. "Nothing small about me. What are your plans for the afternoon?"

"I thought we might give Kamoana a tour of the resort," Beatrice said, still grinning. "The gardens, the trails, and the ballroom."

"Ooh!" Eddi gulped down a large bite of brownie and said, "Prince Mike, the Summer Ball is this weekend. Kamoana has a gorgeous dress."

"I look forward to seeing it." Mike laid his forearm along the back of my chair, gazed down at me, and spoke in a melting tone. "You'll enjoy dancing with me."

I gave Beatrice a desperate look. She caught my eye and asked brightly, "What would you most like to do this afternoon, Kamoana?"

"Could we take out a boat? I'm not used to being away from water for so long."

"Sure! Let's go get ready."

And we three girls tossed our serviettes on the table and rushed (or, in my case, tottered) for the door. Taking pity on me,

Beatrice headed for the elevator again, and I used the break to rub my aching legs and feet.

I was destined for disappointment. When we arrived at the docks, clad once again for swimming and sunbathing, we were told that every boat was checked out or reserved for the day. "What can we do instead?" I asked. I wasn't keen on walking anywhere; it required too much concentration.

"You can sit on the beach with me," Mike announced from behind us. There was just no escaping the man. Why couldn't he hang out with some of the women who wanted him around?

Eddi, at least, was enthusiastic, and we were dressed for nothing else, so we followed him to the beach. Almost as soon as we got there, Eddi found friends her age and settled in to talk.

I had my own coverup gown now, a pretty yellow one to match my suit. I slipped it off, but soon I put it back on again. Beatrice and Eddi both wore swimsuits that covered their midsections, but Mother had given me what Eddi called a "bikini." I didn't dislike the way I looked in it as much as I disliked the way other people looked when they looked at me. Especially Mike.

Ignoring his attempts to draw me into conversation, I put glasses with dark lenses on my face—they really did cut down the sun's glare—tipped my broad-brimmed hat forward, deliberately tightened the belt of my coverup, wishing it were longer, and lay back in a reclining chair made mostly of fabric. The sun was hot on my legs, and sweat trickled down my neck from beneath my hat. I had often sat on Siren Rock with my sisters and watched them call unwary men to crash on the rocks, but there we'd had waves dashing up at us and a breeze to keep us cool. Here, the lake was too far away, I was surrounded by humans, and the air felt heavy.

When I couldn't take it anymore, I sat up and looked around. Mike sprawled in a chair on my left, shirtless again, and Beatrice sat reading a book on my right. She always looked ladylike, no matter the setting, no matter what she wore. Her features individually weren't exceptional, yet she had a peaceful beauty that came from within. I wished for even half her poise.

Children ran about and played in the shallow water, closely watched by a lifeguard. Several adults floated in the marked swimming area, and a few men played a game in the water with a ball and nets. Many people simply soaked up sunlight or talked while they baked.

Yet even now I felt people watching me. Possibly half of them were watching Mike, but I still felt the attention and disliked it intensely. My life had always been private. The beach was anything but private.

Sensing a focused gaze, or something more, I turned to my left. A group of people stood at the edge of the beach: two women talking and two men wearing dark glasses. As soon as I turned their way, one of the men said something, and one of the women smiled and waved at me. I quickly glanced at my companions, but they were either distracted or asleep. When the smiling woman beckoned to me, I quietly stood up, brushed off sand, and said, "I'm going to walk about a bit."

Beatrice shaded her eyes and looked up to give me a nod, Mike snored, and Eddi was too focused on her friends to even hear me.

Carefully I picked my way between sunbathers and approached the strangers.

The friendly woman, who looked my age or younger, came to meet me, her face glowing with excitement. "Are you Kamoana? Say you are! They all think I'm crazy, but I recognize your face."

She was a total stranger to me. I glanced toward the others and sensed magic in the group but wasn't sure from which of them it came. The other woman was probably in her late thirties, and her eyes had an evaluating look. The men had light skin and appeared younger. The taller one had hair growing on his face; the other one's chin was smooth. Reflective lenses hid their eyes.

"My name is Kamoana. But how do you know me?"

"Yes!" The girl pumped her fist. "I knew it!" She was tall, square-shouldered, and strong, with dark skin, a cloud of curly black hair, and a smile that seemed to stretch from ear to ear. "I'm Nora, Nora Rachid, and you saved my life about a month ago. You saved all of us!"

"I beg your pardon?" My mind felt blank.

Her companions, who stood near enough to hear us, looked uncomfortable. The hairy-faced tall man said something to the woman, then walked off toward the docks without another glance at me.

"Aren't you a mermaid?" Nora had the presence of mind to lower her voice while she asked, but I still felt irked.

"Do I look like a mermaid?" I asked.

Her smile dimmed. "You don't have a tail, but you're just as gorgeous as I thought, and every man on the beach is trying not to stare at you. Most of them are failing."

I felt my face go even hotter than the sun had made it.

Her eyes behind those thick lenses became intense. "I watched you at lunch. You don't know how to use silverware, and the food was all new to you. How long have you been in human form?"

I wilted. "Since this morning. Do you think everyone here knows?"

She laughed in triumph, then shook her head. "Most people here aren't looking for a mermaid. Not that I was looking for one in the dining hall. I happened to recognize your face when you walked in. My aunt thought I was being ridiculous, but now . . ."

Nora turned and beckoned her friends forward. "Where did Tor go?" she asked as the two approached, but kept talking without waiting for an answer. "I was right, it is her! She might not recognize us, but how could anyone forget her face?"

She indicated the woman with a little wave. "Kamoana, this is my aunt, Dr. Saliha Benyamina, associate professor of Oceanic Sciences, Magical and Natural, at the University of Barbacha; and this is Jonathan Howell, her research assistant who's working on a master's degree. Aunt Saliha and Jonathan, you know Kamoana the mermaid, though I don't recall any formal introductions being made during the confusion in the lifeboat." She looked around, craning her neck, and asked again, "Where did Tor run off to? He's been acting so strange . . ."

"He's claiming our boat," Dr. Benyamina said, her tone subdued as she studied me up and down. She looked nothing like her niece. Slim yet muscular, with delicate features, glossy black hair held captive in a bun, and skin like brown silk, she might have been a fitness model. Without doubt, she was the source of the low-grade magic I had sensed. "Hello, Kamoana," she said. "We had planned to hunt for the mermaid—you—in the lake today. Do you take human form often? I should imagine such a change requires a great deal of magic."

Nora snorted. "If she took human form often, she would know how to use a fork by now!" Then she pulled in her lips, gave her head a shake, and amended, "Sorry, Kamoana! That was rude. You did great for a first try at using silverware."

While the women were talking, Jonathan Howell had pulled off his sunglasses to reveal big brown eyes that studied me with eager interest. He tried to speak, had to clear his throat twice, then said, "I must say, I still can't believe it. I mean, I've studied merfolk for a few years now, but the best any collections and museums have to offer are ancient specimens, unverified stories of encounters, and questionable artifacts. Then, boom! Our research boat swamps in a storm off the coast of Barbacha, and a siren scoops us into a lifeboat. A siren!" His voice trembled with either excitement or nerves. Maybe both.

I tried to look pleasant but felt all kinds of awkward. They all talked to me yet allowed me no opportunity to answer. Even now they chatted together about the storm . . . the shipwreck.

Their words stirred up that cloudy feeling in my head, but no memories came this time. These humans knew my name and face, so it must have happened: Only a month ago I'd been in the Begaian Sea. Why couldn't I remember? Surely Mother hadn't stolen my memories of everything connected to humans, so this storm, these people, must be a clue to my mystery.

While they reminisced about the horrors of nearly drowning and how they hadn't seen me until I spoke to them, I considered Jonathan Howell as a possible love interest. He was an ocean scientist interested in magical sea creatures, and he was better-looking up close than from a distance. Several inches taller than me, with pale skin, a stocky build, glossy brown hair like a mink's fur, and cheeks that dented in when he smiled.

When I gave him a brief smile, his face lit up. He didn't make my heart go pitter-pat, but I decided he could be a contender.

Dr. Benyamina cleared her throat. "Kamoana, if you live here, may I ask why you were in the Begaian Sea that day?"

When I didn't immediately answer, Nora jumped in. "I thought maybe you came to see Tor. Since you know each other." My expression must have been blank, for her brow wrinkled, and she blurted, "Wait, you don't even recognize him? Torbjørn, Lord Magnussen of Hyllestad?"

I slowly shook my head. Why would I have been in the Begaian . . . Oh, wait! The annual Siren Song Ball was located there last month in the sunken city of Kranakoa . . . I glimpsed a flicker of dancing merfolk . . .

Then a crushing pain filled my head, probably the spell smashing down any memories that tried to break free. Squeezing my eyes shut, I inwardly railed at my mother. Why had she thrown me into this embarrassing position?

6

I 'M SO SORRY," I said, "but since I turned human, I'm having memory issues." I felt Dr. Benyamina's assessing stare and wished I could slide into the lake and disappear.

"Do you often switch forms?" Jonathan asked eagerly. "We didn't know merfolk could change into human shape. This is a groundbreaking discovery! How is it done? Do you always lose memories when you change shape?"

I glanced back toward my empty beach chair. Beatrice was still reading, Eddi had wandered off, and Mike now sat upright and was stretching his arms while nearby women gaped in awe. "I . . . um . . . No, I don't often switch forms." I attempted another smile.

Dr. Benyamina's eyes narrowed. She seemed too young to be a professor at a university, let alone Nora's aunt, but her eyes were disconcertingly analytical. "May I ask why you changed forms this time?"

I didn't want to answer, but my mouth opened anyway. Just in time, I realized she had placed a compulsion on me and said only, "I have a mission to accomplish."

The doctor's fine brows rose high.

Nora let out a breathy sigh. "This is way beyond cool!"

I, for one, was fed up with being magically manipulated. "I'm thankful you're all safe and healthy," I began, taking a step back, "and I wish you—"

"We have a ski boat rented for the next two hours, just to drive around and see the lake. Tor promised to give us a tour," the doctor interrupted me. "I do hope you will join us."

Again I felt a slight magical tug. I could easily resist it now, yet the prospect of a boat cruise overrode my misgivings. The water had been calling to me all day. "Oh! I . . ." I glanced over my shoulder to see Beatrice looking our way. Mike was talking with three pretty girls. "Can my friends join us?"

"Are your friends merfolk too?" Nora asked eagerly.

"Um, no, I just met them this morning."

She beamed her friendly smile. "No matter. The boat holds eight adults, they said. Plenty of room."

I saw her eyes cut toward Mike and inwardly groaned, thinking, *Girl, raise your standards!*

The doctor gave Jonathan a certain look, and he asked, "So, do your friends know your true identity? We won't tell anyone."

"They do. No worries. I'll go ask them about a boat ride. And thanks!"

"We'll meet you at the dock," he said, and those intriguing dents reappeared on his cheeks when he smiled.

"I'll hurry!"

While the scholars walked toward the docks, I approached Beatrice. "I've been invited on a boat ride with those people from some university. Would you like to join us?"

She shaded her eyes with one hand and squinted up at me. "You don't sound entirely thrilled about it. Do you want us to come?"

I suddenly felt confused. I wanted my friends to come along. Yet I didn't. My mouth opened, but nothing came out. I couldn't blame any magical influence—this was my own indecision.

Beatrice's face scrunched. "Are you all right, Kamoana? Who are those people?"

Eddi appeared from behind me. "They're Lord Magnussen's friends from his university and some lady professor. My friend Maria says they're eggheads who talk about fish all the time." Without a pause she gave Beatrice the pleading eyes. "May I go kayaking with Maria and Ianthe? I promise to stay close to shore and break no rules."

"Sure, go ahead."

Grinning, Eddi squeezed her eyes shut, said, "Thanks, 'Mom' Bea!" then turned to me. "Have fun with your brainboxes, Kamoana! Maybe they want to study you." With that, she spun about and ran off again.

Beatrice nodded at me. "You go on ahead. I slathered on sunblock, my hat's doing its job, this book is pretty good, and I need to be here when the flighty princess returns. We'll come by your room before dinner, okay? Even if you're bored to tears on the boat ride, you can check two men off your list of possibilities."

She had a point. "Thanks!" I picked up my purse, gave her a wave, and headed toward the little marina, dodging a few men who stepped into my path with obvious intent to delay. "Excuse me, please!" I repeated several times.

I tried to walk fast, but I was still unsteady on my feet. Even with shoes, my feet seemed to find every rock. Worst of all, my repurposed bones and muscles screamed at me to stop this torturous motion. Nevertheless, I felt pleased with my rapid progress since morning.

My own magic helped, of course. Only rarely do merfolk have power beyond that of *burvae*, humans with the second-lowest level of magic, and most of the magic we do have is focused on water-centric skills. Siren-calling, for instance. Although I possess no remarkable magical abilities, I've always found ways to repurpose what I've got.

However, sometimes I feel as if my magic is busily doing something in my subconscious mind, which can be unnerving.

Once I reached the docks, I scanned the scene until I located the university group toward the end of the second dock. They had rented the resort's oldest ski boat, one my sisters had never yet managed to wreck. The professor sat in the driver's seat, with Jonathan on the seat across from hers. Those two conversed while Nora and the hairy-faced man—Tor? Lord Magnussen?—untied the mooring lines. His back was to me as he squatted on the dock.

"Kamoana!" Nora, on the dock at the boat's stern, stood upright and waved. "See, Tor? She came."

Waving back, I forgot to pay attention to my feet. Just as Tor started to turn around, the toe of my sneaker caught on the dock. I then tripped over my own feet, arms flailing, and for a horrible instant thought I would fall right into the man. Desperate to avoid a collision, I grasped for the boat, but my hand shoved it away from the dock, and for a second horrible instant I looked straight down at water.

Yes, my stomach dropped at the thought of falling into the lake. How ironic is that?

A large hand caught my arm, pulled me upright, steadied me, then let go and joined another hand on the mooring line to haul the boat back to the dock. Standing as if frozen, I watched as the bow slid toward me while Jonathan sprang to the dock and hurried over to grin down at me. "Not so steady on those feet yet, are you?"

Slowly, carefully, I turned to look at the tall man holding the mooring line. He still wore those reflective glasses, so my only real impression of his face was of strong cheekbones, a flat-lined mouth, and that short beard. He wore a cap with its bill turned backwards, and there was white stuff smeared all over his nose. "Thank you," I said. "Do you mind if I come along for the boat ride?" My voice sounded weak and fearful.

Jonathan answered, "Why would he mind having a beautiful woman join our cruise?" I studied Tor while Jonathan chattered on: "There's plenty of room. Tor's the only one of us who's been to the resort before—we three aren't noble, rich, or royal. I think every lifeguard in the place has warned us not to let him drive, but he might be useful to tell us what he knows about the lake."

I could only assume Tor was looking back at me. I hate reflective sunglasses—my distorted reflection stared back at me from both lenses, all wide eyes and huge nose. Then that grim mouth opened, and Tor said, "You must know far more about the lake than I do." He tossed the line aboard and held the boat close to the dock with both hands. "Climb aboard."

I wanted to say something clever and amusing. My weak "thank you" just didn't cut it.

Jonathan helped me climb in and then sat beside me in the back. Nora sat at my other side. I found my own sunglasses in the pocket of my cover-up and shoved them onto my face.

People couldn't tell where I was looking while I hid behind those reflective lenses. And people couldn't instantly know what I was thinking.

People . . . Tor, that is, climbed aboard while the doctor backed the boat away from the dock. With his back to us, he pulled off his cap and ran his hand over short-cropped brown hair.

Soon I felt lake wind in my face and hair. The spray was refreshing, yet I felt a heaviness in my chest. It couldn't be because that man seemed to despise me. Why should his opinion matter when just about every other unattached human male clamored for my attention? Why should I care? It wasn't because of his looks or manners. He was sullen, and the hairy face and that greasy white smear on his nose didn't improve matters.

"Have you ever been in a boat before, Kamoana?" Nora asked. "I mean, you jumped into our lifeboat when you rescued us, but that wasn't anything like this."

A flash of lightning filled my brain, revealing mountainous waves and a nearly swamped boat holding two people. I rubbed my aching temples and couldn't answer.

"The monster!" Jonathan said, his voice eager. "Nobody's said a word about the sea monster that helped you rescue us. Does it live in the Begaian Sea? You never did say why you were there that day."

I met his curious gaze, then turned my head to meet Nora's. Tor stared out across the lake, and the professor kept her eyes forward as we skimmed over its surface. I wasn't sure whether those two could hear our conversation. "A sea monster was at the rescue?" I asked.

"Yes," Nora said. "A giant serpent-thing. You really don't remember anything! Did you get a concussion too?"

I blinked at her and pulled flying hair out of my face. "I don't think so. What is a concussion?"

"A blow to the head can knock a person unconscious. Sometimes it makes holes in the memories. That's what happened to Tor, we think. Sort of a delayed reaction or something."

Tor shook his head briefly without looking our way. He was a puzzle.

"My memory loss has a different cause," I said vaguely. "If you like, I'll call the monster. You might want to cover your ears."

"Call the monster?" Jonathan asked. "Wait! It's here in the lake?"

I closed my eyes, opened my mouth, and used siren magic to amplify my voice. "Nelumbo! Are you near?"

Hearing yelps around me, I opened my eyes to see the four scholars cringing, their hands over their ears. The boat slowed quickly, for the professor could no longer steer. She threw me an angry glance and snapped, "You should have given us a clearer warning!"

"I'm terribly sorry. I . . . I don't usually use that voice above water." I glanced at each of the others in turn. Would they all hate me now?

Nora was wide-eyed but gave me a crooked grin, still rubbing her ears. Jonathan had fallen away from me and still leaned on the end of our bench seat, also rubbing his ears. Tor had spun around to face me but didn't say a word. His expression was still bleak, but he didn't look angry.

Nora laughed shakily. "Easy on the eyes, hard on the ears," she said. "Aren't you glad I'm the opposite, Tor?"

His lips twitched, the first softness I'd seen on that face. "You're not hard on the eyes, Nora," he said. "Don't be so down on yourself."

I wondered if they were a couple. Two odd intellectuals who had bonded over fish and a shipwreck? Or maybe just good friends. She didn't look at all starry-eyed.

I turned to Jonathan. "I'm truly sorry."

He straightened on the seat and gave me a faint smile. "It's all right. You're a lot more considera—" His voice broke off and his eyes went wide, staring past me.

Hearing the rush of water, I turned around. "Hello, Nelumbo."

The lake serpent gave me a quick glance in passing. He was still rising out of the water—the creature enjoyed making an impression. Water dripped from the fleshy growths on his head and the bristling spikes down his back; his scales glittered in the sunlight. He was hideous, truth be told, but I had always loved the silly creature.

The four scholars recoiled, and I couldn't blame them. "You don't need to show off, Nelumbo," I called up at him. "According to my friends here, you've met them all before. Do you remember a shipwreck in the Begaian Sea?"

He curved back around, and his yellow eyes peered more closely at my companions, his chin dripping water that soaked the boat's carpeting. Jonathan swore under his breath and squished himself as far back in the seat as he could go. Nora crouched on the floor and stared up at the beast as though mesmerized. The professor clapped both hands over her face and peered between her fingers, cowering.

Tor, however, sat upright in his seat and stared at the serpent, his face still expressionless.

"I remember the lake monster," I heard him say. "I remember . . ."

7

THE SERPENT TILTED his huge head to one side and shook it slightly, showering us with more water. He then lowered it to look directly into Tor's face, and his mouth opened in a grin that revealed rows of greenish-black, dagger-like teeth. Tor stood up, lifted one hand, and laid it on one of the spikes projecting from the monster's snout. For a human, even I had to admit, that took some guts.

Dr. Benyamina huddled in a ball on her seat, hands over her head, swearing and praying with vehement incoherence. "Make it go away!" she wailed.

"Nelumbo," I said. "Perhaps you'd better back off a bit. What's the use in saving these humans from drowning if you frighten them to death?"

His grin widened, but he pulled back and did a backward dive, his belly arching before us, silvery scales flashing past until his tail appeared, arched over, and vanished beneath the waves. I had never understood how he managed to leave almost no ripple on the surface.

I looked around at the scholars. "Nelumbo knows you, and I have vague memories of a storm and a shipwreck." Maybe when I had a chance to focus, the flickering images would coalesce into a memory. "I must have been in the Begaian Sea to attend the annual merfolk dance, the Siren Song Ball." I paused, then added, "Although I generally avoid formal occasions."

"Mermaids dance?" Nora asked from her place on the floor.

"Yes. We have a rich musical tradition and history. I mean, we're sirens! We sometimes copy human music, but it doesn't usually go well, since water and air carry sound differently." Faraway Castle frequently hosted casual dances on the lakeshore, and I had been known to spy on the humans.

Regaining her courage and reclaiming the wheel, Dr. Benyamina gunned the idling engine, and we were on our way.

Nora resumed her seat, and Jonathan again sat upright, brushing off his shirt in an attempt to look casual. "You say the serpent has never harmed anyone?" he asked after a pensive pause.

"Never, although there is one prince he dislikes and torments whenever the poor fellow approaches the lake," I said with a smile. "He truly isn't dangerous to guests. I don't know how he behaves when he's out in the oceans of the world, but I've never heard that he makes trouble." I nearly told them that my mother would handle any misdemeanors, but something made me hold my tongue. These humans already knew too much about me.

I saw Palau Kalah ahead of us and quickly growing larger. Boats were forbidden to approach my home island, but the professor drove closer than most dared.

Sheer cliffs composed this north shore of the island, and lumps of hardened lava rose from the waves lapping on the rocks. Seabirds dived off those rocks, hunting fish. The water immediately around Palau Kalah was ocean water, part of the magical pocket that held the island in place. As the boat turned and cruised along the west shore, hidden from the castle by the island's bulk, I explained these details, adding, "The volcano hasn't erupted for a few years, but some of those pillars of lava rock happened during my lifetime." It was ten years now since my father died and Mt. Ibu erupted, expressing my mother's devastation.

"I don't see any sirens on the rocks," Jonathan said. "Are there any? I mean, are they invisible?"

"You would see them if they were there," I said. "You can see most magical creatures ever since I spoke to you."

"Yeah, we can see all those little brown people swarming in the dining hall and lobby." He grimaced. "I guess most of the guests can't."

I felt uncomfortable. "The magic is hard to explain, and I don't have the power to reverse it." Mother could but seldom bothered to.

"I think brownies are cute," Nora said.

While those two discussed brownies, dwarfs, and sirens, I watched the shore of my island skim past. It had a deserted look, the lagoon, the beaches, the rocks.

"So why aren't any sirens around?" Nora asked me directly. "I thought there were always sirens on the island."

"They have busy lives away from this lake," I said, "in other bodies of water. My sisters are all married now. Coral has little ones at home, and Talulah is a newlywed. Moselle visits most often, but never alone. Sirens like to talk." I didn't bother mentioning that my current state must horrify my sisters. They would not want to see me in human shape; they didn't even like seeing our mother that way.

As we cruised around the island, I realized that my feelings about this spell were undergoing a sea change. Truth be told, I found the experience rather fascinating. I had adjusted to the humans' appearance more quickly than I might have expected. Beatrice and Eddi were my friends. Nora was fun. Jonathan seemed nice. My gaze flicked to the back of Tor's head, then to Dr. Benyamina's neat bun. I wasn't so sure how I felt about those two.

"Tell us about the lake?" Jonathan requested just then, reclaiming my attention. Sunglasses hid his eyes, but those intriguing dents were in plain sight when he smiled.

"Why do your cheeks dent when you smile?" I asked outright.

His brows rose high. "Dent?"

Nora laughed. "Those are dimples. He's tremendously proud of them."

"But why do they happen?" I persisted.

He shrugged a thick shoulder. "They're hereditary. My father has dimples. I inherited that gene. Don't merpeople ever have them?"

"Not that I've seen."

"It's a defect," Nora said, her tone serious. "So sad."

I knew better than to believe that. "I like it," I said.

"Doesn't every woman like dimples on a man?" Nora's dark eyes laughed, and I couldn't help smiling back. "But now, please do tell us about Faraway Lake. We're scientists; we want to know everything."

I thought for a moment. "Faraway Lake is quite large for a mountain lake, and it is protected by magic to be safe for resort guests. Water runs into it in streams and waterfalls on all sides, and it empties into only one large stream to the southeast, not very far from the castle. That outlet is magically protected so that nothing except fish can get through in either direction. The resort is a haven for many endangered birds and fish, since there is no shooting or fishing allowed."

"So how do you get to other bodies of water from here?" Nora asked.

"We have magical ways of moving about," I said. "All merfolk do."

"Do magical creatures often appear in the lake?" Dr. Benyamina called out this question without turning around.

"None besides merfolk and Nelumbo."

"I suppose he chases any others away," Jonathan said.

"He probably would, if any showed up." My mother was the real deterrent, but these people didn't need to know that.

Again the professor called over her shoulder. "Do any magical fish live in the lake?"

"None that I know of, although some are unusually smart." Speaking of smart fish made me miss my special pet, Fathoms, a catfish I had rescued from illegal fishermen years ago. Did he know I was riding around in this boat, maybe passing directly above him?

Tor turned in his seat to face us. "There's a giant catfish living in the middle of the lake." His deep voice had a raspy edge.

"Have you seen the Grandfather Fish?" I asked in genuine surprise.

"I have." He paused, looking puzzled. "Can't recall how that came about." He growled the last words, then faced forward in his seat and stretched one long arm over the side to catch spray.

It made sense that a few resort guests had seen the huge catfish over the years. I didn't want to make too much of this. But Tor's loss of memory seemed nearly as specific as mine.

"Have you seen him?" I asked Jonathan. "The Grandfather Fish, I mean?"

He smiled again. "This is my first time on Faraway Lake. Tor's been here for a week, but we three arrived last night. We're here as his visitors for a few days—Nora talked me into coming along."

"No, I didn't." Nora laughed aloud. "You are just as siren-crazed as Tor."

I found this statement puzzling. Neither man acted enthralled. Jonathan obviously admired me, but Tor almost seemed repelled.

Nora turned to me. "When you rescued Tor, you must have told him you lived in Faraway Lake. He told us we had to come here, and he got permission to bring in guests."

Jonathan added, "None of us got to thank you properly for saving our lives at the time, and this place sounded like something we all should see, since our specialty is magical marine life—and 'aquatic' really should be fitted into the title. All water life is our thing."

"I'm so glad we came," Nora said with frank appreciation. "We're already chatting like old friends with a real siren, and we got to see the giant serpent in full daylight. Who knows what other surprises lie ahead?"

"Why would I have told Tor that I live in Faraway Lake?" I asked, glancing at his back. Sunlight glinted gold on his short hair. He faced front, but I knew he was listening to us.

"Maybe he asked?" Nora said. "He was the last one into the lifeboat. I think he was nearest to drowning after that blow to his head. Maybe you talked to keep him awake? He was shouting and thrashing."

Frowning, Jonathan added, "When you tried to leave, he jumped into the ocean after you."

My face felt hot, and I couldn't help glancing at Tor again. "I don't remember enthralling anyone," I said, trying to ease the tension, "but if I did siren-call by mistake, Tor's behavior wasn't his fault."

"Huh," Jonathan said. "I was completely dazzled, but I didn't swim after you or cry when you were gone."

Was he implying that Tor had done those things? I could not begin to imagine it!

"Oh really?" Nora said with heavy irony. "As I recall, Jonathan, you hardly spoke for the next two days, and then you talked Aunt Saliha into making this trip."

Sometime while we were talking, my island had dropped behind. The ski boat now cruised across a broad open stretch of water. I pulled off my hat before the wind could steal it. My sunglasses cut down the sun's glare on the waves and, I hoped, allowed me to steal glances unnoticed.

Nora stood up, balancing easily in the speeding boat. "I'm headed to the bow for more fresh air," she said. "Coming, Kamoana?"

"Yes!" I grasped at the chance, then recalled my manners. "In a moment." I turned back to Jonathan, whose expression was unreadable, and I spoke clearly: "I don't enthrall humans on purpose. If I enthralled either you or Tor, it was a mistake, and I'm truly sorry." I dared a glance at Tor's back. No response. Maybe he couldn't hear us above the engine, the water, and the wind.

When I started to rise and follow Nora, Jonathan caught hold of my wrist, so I sat back down. His smile had disappeared, and he glanced toward his taciturn friend while speaking for my ears only: "Tor is one of those brilliant but not entirely balanced people, you know? For as long as I've known him, he's focused on his work. He never talks about his private life, but I've gotten the impression he was disappointed in love." He glanced toward Nora's back as she moved to the front.

"You mean, he and Nora . . . ?"

Jonathan's lips quirked. "They say they're just friends, but . . . you know how it is."

I didn't have a clue.

He shrugged. "She's like a little sister to me, and her aunt is . . . well, mostly like a drill sergeant." He whispered the last few words next to my ear: "I was joking earlier—I know you didn't siren-call us. I would love to spend some time with you while I'm here. To learn about lake creatures, of course." He winked.

What did the wink mean? I gave Jonathan a faint smile and looked away. I wanted to follow Nora, but I would have to climb over Tor's legs to reach that door. Nora didn't seem to give it a thought, and he'd ignored her.

The others must wonder what we were muttering about. Nora, in the bow, hung one hand over the side to catch the spray. Tor rested an arm on the side of the boat, and his head was tipped back slightly. Maybe I was missing something, but I detected no attraction between those two despite Jonathan's hints to the contrary. But then, I was no expert on romance . . . or on humans.

As the boat roared along the north shore, I spotted a certain bay. Jonathan wanted to learn about lake creatures, so . . ."My favorite kind of duck nests there," I said, pointing.

Jonathan laughed. "Duck? Did you hear that, Tor?" he called. "She's a bird watcher."

No response. Dr. Benyamina cast me a quick glance over her shoulder, but I couldn't read her expression.

"What's wrong with liking ducks?" I asked. Jonathan was getting on my nerves, hinting at things I didn't understand, never saying what he meant.

He shook his head and grinned. "Nothing. It's just that Tor has a master's degree in ornithology as well as in ichthyology. We're always razzing him about birds, and then you mention duck nests."

I wrapped my fingers around my upper arms. In my private cave under the island, on a shelf above the high-tide line, I kept a stash of books and scientific journals, many of them about birds. One of them featured articles and photos of my favorite duck, a rare variety that had only recently begun to nest at Faraway Lake.

Despite the bright sunlight, I suddenly felt chilled. "I think I'll go join Nora." I was willing to step over Tor's legs to order escape Jonathan's company. I'd heard enough confusing information.

Carefully I walked forward, and Tor moved his legs out of my way. Soon I sat across from Nora and heaved a relieved sigh. Wind pulled my hair loose and whipped it around my face and body.

"This place is so beautiful," Nora called to me across the bow. "I can hardly believe it's real!" She pointed at a tall pine growing alone on a spit of land, then waved toward the snow-capped mountains rising behind it. "Everything is magnificent and feels . . . magical."

I looked at that tree and instantly felt spinning memory clouds in my head. I thought I saw a gigantic bird wheel in the sky above the pine tree, spiraling down . . . My hands came up to my face, and I shuddered. How real it seemed, yet no bird was there!

Sensing . . . something, I turned quickly—and through the water-dotted windscreen I saw Tor's sunglasses. He was looking straight at me.

8

WHILE THE PROFESSOR steered the boat into its berth and the two guys jumped onto the dock to tie it up, I saw shirtless Mike walking toward the docks, his smile shedding light on every female in its radius.

Great. Just great.

"Do you still want me to dine with your group tonight?" I asked Nora hopefully.

"Sure, that'd be awesome," she answered with her friendly smile, then followed my gaze. "Is there any way I could get you to introduce me to Mr. Too-Gorgeous-for-Words? Or is he yours?"

"I'll gladly introduce you if you'll take him off my hands," I answered, my voice loud enough for nearby people to hear. "His name is Mike, he's a prince, and he'll tell you he's irresistible."

Nora laughed. "I won't argue with that! I would say he's my type, but I'm guessing he's every woman's type."

"He's not my type, I can tell you that much." My tone was dry. I couldn't resist a glance at Tor. He finished tying off the boat and walked away without a word or glance for anyone.

"All the better for me." Nora watched Mike approach. "In my dreams, anyway."

Jonathan helped Dr. Benyamina off the boat, and she hauled him aside to talk right there on the dock.

Mike crossed paths with Tor as if he didn't exist, then paused beside the boat. "Kamoana, my sweet, I have a wonderful surprise for you. C'mon. I'll lift you down." He held up one hand to me, striking a pose that showed off every muscle in his arms and torso.

"First you need to meet my friends," I said, trying to sound cheery. "Dr. Benyamina, this is Prince Michael. Mike, the lovely doctor. And this is Jonathan Howell." Startled, those two returned polite greetings, then moved toward the shore, still talking.

Nora leaned over the side of the boat and almost flung her hand at Mike. "Nora. Miss Nora Rachid."

Mike took her hand and nodded, gazing into her eyes. "Miss Rachid, I am honored." He turned and caught my eye, bent gracefully to press a kiss to the inside of Nora's wrist, then slanted another look at me. No doubt hoping I'd be jealous.

Nora gaped, and for a moment I thought she might swoon. But then she laughed aloud. "I love it! You must practice that before a mirror. Too funny!"

Mike jerked upright, dropping her hand. "Practice before a mirror? I beg your pardon."

"No need to apologize. I liked it." She climbed out of the boat, and he was too thunderstruck to help her. She boldly slipped her hand into the bend of his elbow and smiled up at him. "Walk me back?"

He blinked. "Uh . . . Sure." It was weak, but he was committed. As they walked along the dock to the beach, I donned my hat and climbed over the boat's side. Fearing Mike would look back, I hurried to a storage shed halfway along the dock, slipped inside, then peered around the doorframe. Mike and Nora strolled past the beach and toward the castle, chatting with animation. I couldn't see the other three scholars anywhere.

I heaved a sigh and stepped back. Someone gently grasped my elbows to stop me. With a startled yelp I spun around and stared into the dim shed, then up to meet my reflection in a pair of sunglasses. I pulled off my own glasses to see him more clearly, then put them back on, feeling safer that way. "I'm sorry! I was . . . um . . ." I couldn't think what to say.

"Hiding?" Tor supplied, standing amid a collection of fins and masks and rubber suits. He seemed to fill the shed.

"You were too," I guessed, and took a step back.

I saw both annoyance and humor flash across his face. "Possibly." He stared out the door above my head. "Nice hand-off, out there."

"Hand-off?"

"Transfer. Like when a sports player hands off the ball to a teammate."

"Oh. Right. Nora played her part well." The man had a sense of humor? "And everyone is happier this way," I added for good measure. Did his lips twitch? Feeling reckless, I squared off. "Jonathan says you study birds. Do you know that goldeneye ducks have started nesting on Faraway Lake?"

He still gazed over my head. "Are you sure they're goldeneyes?"

"Pretty sure." I matched his dry tone. "Their eyes are golden."

One side of his mouth and one brow pulled upward. "But are they ducks?"

"I forgot to ask, but they quack like ducks."

This time his brief smile showed teeth. "Sounds promising."

"If you like, I could take you and your friends to that bay tomorrow for a look."

"They won't be interested in ducks."

But was he interested? "It's not as if finding a few ducks would take much time. Afterward we could all go snorkeling around the island, and they could see the saltwater fish."

His smile vanished. "The forbidden island where sirens lurk." His tone went flat, but he looked down at me, his eyes still hidden. I hoped my glasses concealed my eyes as thoroughly; it was only fair.

"The very one. My home. We can sneak around to the back side, drop people off, then leave the boat hidden somewhere. Please come! The fish around the island are worth seeing. And maybe my catfish friend will show up. He's nearly four feet long and does tricks." I had little hope of enticing this frowning man, but something prompted me to keep talking.

I hated talking at my reflection in his glasses, but I saw indecision in the way his mouth moved. "I'll ask the others if they're interested," he said grudgingly.

"Mention that I could ask Nelumbo to join us if they want to see him again," I said. "Nora invited me to sit with you all at dinner tonight, so I'll add my direct invitation then." Tardily I remembered: "But my friends Miss Beatrice and Princess Edurne might be expecting me, so I'm not sure that will happen."

"There are tables to seat eight, even ten."

His gruff statement surprised me into silence. Briefly. "Yes, but . . ." I hesitated.

He came through for me. "Invite your friends to join us. Or us to join your friends."

After studying his face a moment longer, I smiled. "Thank you. I will. See you then." I turned and hurried toward the castle, walking with great care just in case he was watching. Halfway there, I found Beatrice and Eddi, along with a young dwarf wearing a glamour that made him appear human. He gave me a wary look. Did Eddi not know he was a dwarf?

"Did you have a good boat ride?" Beatrice asked as I fell in step with the group.

"I did!" I even gave a little skip, tripped, and staggered a few steps. My feet weren't light, but my heart was buoyant for the time being. "Who's your friend, Eddi?"

"This is Kai," she said. "We've been friends forever. I mean, every summer I come to the castle. He works here."

"Pleased to meet you, Kai." I gave him a genuine smile— careful to meet the eyes of his projected image, located a bit higher than his real eyes—and he visibly relaxed, returning my greeting with excellent manners.

"Pleased to meet you, Your Highness."

"What? Are you a princess too? You didn't tell us!" Eddi exclaimed, then turned on Kai. "How did you know?"

My face felt warm. "I guess it never came up. My mother is Queen Pukai."

That name meant nothing to the girls, but Kai nodded respectfully. I noticed he didn't try to answer Eddi's question. The dwarfs who worked at the castle must all know about my mother.

"We must start introducing you properly," Beatrice said in her gentle way. "But don't worry, we'll still call you Kamoana if you prefer."

"I definitely prefer. And Kai, you may call me by name too, all right?"

He gave me a shy smile.

As Eddi and Kai moved on ahead, Beatrice turned to me with eager interest. "I have something to tell you, but you look so energized! You talk first: Do you think one of those scientist men is the right one?"

My heart gave an extra thump. "I'm not sure, but it could be . . . We're to join them for dinner tonight, or they might join us, if you don't mind. And we might be going on a snorkeling trek out to Palau Kalah tomorrow morning!"

"To where?"

"Palau Kalah—my mother's island. It is surrounded by ocean water, so those marine-studies people should love it! We'll find a way to keep from being seen. If anyone ever knew how to sneak around, I'm the girl."

Beatrice blinked and tried to smile. "It . . . it sounds amazing, really! Your mother won't mind?"

I shrugged. "She's the one who turned me human. If I come back as a human to torment her, it's no more than she deserves."

"I'm not sure if Eddi and I are free tomorrow, but I'll let you know soon. So . . ." Beatrice sounded tentative. "You really liked this guy? I mean, are you sure? What's his name?"

"I'm not sure he's the guy, and I don't know whether I like him or not." My euphoria dimmed. Was I more excited about the man or about thwarting my mother's plans? "I forgot you haven't met any of them. His name is Tor. Lord . . . Mag-something."

Her eyes widened. "Oh! Lord Magnussen. Oh, my! You've already met him? I was going to tell you."

"Tell me what?" I asked, feeling strangely defensive. I pulled her off the path to let people pass us and asked, "You know him?"

She shook her head. "I've never met him, but there was talk on the beach this morning about a lord who got in major trouble earlier this week. He is banned from renting any equipment, and some people wanted to ban him from even riding in a boat. Rumor says he was enthralled by sirens and landed a ski boat on the island's beach—which no one has ever done before. After he was rescued and supposedly treated by the psychiatrist, he sneaked over to the island again. When a friend followed him, Lord Magnussen smashed the guy's kayak and left him—a prince!—floating in the lake. A lifeguard rescued the prince, but Lord Magnussen didn't come back, and all kinds of rumors were flying. But then he reappeared a few nights ago as if nothing had ever happened. They say he remembers none of it."

As I listened, my heart felt like a stone in my chest. Had he come to see me? Only days ago? Adding this story to Jonathan's offhand description of a man who'd wept and despaired at parting from me painted a portrait of a man nothing like the Tor I'd met today. Had Mother's spell changed his personality? Or—I knew it was the truth as soon as the thought occurred to me—was he confused and angry and embarrassed?

Beatrice looked distressed. "I only heard about it a few minutes ago. One of the lifeguards at the beach today was part of the crew that picked up the grounded ski boat. Lord Magnussen is eccentric, they say. An amazing brain, and no interest in social events. He has a few good friends and a great family, but he really cares only about wildlife."

If Tor had forgotten everything about me as thoroughly as I had forgotten him, he must be even more freaked out by this situation than I was, possibly questioning his own sanity. Yet he had unbent enough to banter with me a little. And he had invited me to join his group for dinner. Standing there on a patch of grass, I looked between trees to glimpse Palau Kalah, glowing like a jewel against the vivid blue water.

"Do you think he went to the island to see me?" I asked. How strange it felt to ask such a question!

Beatrice brushed sand from her ankle. "My thoughts don't really matter, but I must say, everything lines up perfectly. Now you just need to get him to love you all over again and propose. I'm sure you can do it."

"I'm not," I said, my tone flat. "I'm not sure I even want to make the effort." Could that man, a complete stranger, be worth sacrificing my future, my freedom . . . my tail? It didn't seem possible. Yet at one time, a very recent time, I must have thought so. Did I trust myself-of-yesterday enough to take the chance?

Back in my room, alone for the time, I stared out the window at people boating and kayaking on the lake. I kept thinking about my life, my real life. For years I'd been cataloging the fish, birds, and other aquatic creatures of Faraway Lake, and I fully intended to complete the same process with the marine life surrounding Palau Kalah. After that? Entire oceans to explore. My studies gave me joy and fulfillment. Romance and marriage had never been a priority . . . that I could recall.

Resentment burned in my chest. Why had Mother stolen so much of my life from me? Had I made a complete fool of myself with a human? Did everyone in the merworld know about my folly? I could not imagine sacrificing everything I knew and loved for . . . I tried to picture Tor's face but saw only sunglasses, white sunblock, and hair. I'd been so nervous about looking at him that I had only a general impression of a rangy frame and angular features. Yet I also had the strange sense that I could easily pick him out of a crowd of hundreds. Even from a distance.

Stupid spell. How could I make wise decisions now if I lacked vital information about then? Should I respect myself enough to trust my decisions of the past, or should I assume I'd been a fool, chuck the past, and start over with the facts I could recall?

My memories of the past month were few and indistinct, and I also sensed large gaps in my recollections of a few years during my teens. Why? Something significant must have happened back then, again a month ago at the shipwreck, and again early this week.

My head ached when I focused on recalling memories. Exhausted by the useless effort, I lay down on my soft bed and closed my eyes to rest. I couldn't recall the past, but I could freely ponder the gossip Beatrice had relayed to me. Kamoana of a week ago had apparently welcomed this man's invasion of my home not once, but twice. Mother would never have cast this humiliating mess of a spell if I'd rejected him.

No human had ever set foot on Palau Kalah in my lifetime. If he'd done it after my sisters called him, they must have been in a panic. I couldn't help smirking at the thought. I loved all three of them, but they constantly lectured me on how to be a proper siren. As if I cared!

As I lay there, my own magic tingled through my brain, and I fell into a dream. Soft music floated to my ears as I swirled in the arms of a prince at the Siren Song Ball . . .

9

THE BEGAIAN SEA was cool at this depth, and fish darted in and out among the dancers. Even a few sea snakes swirled like striped ribbons, showing off their dance moves. Other couples moved around us, tails and fins swishing, the sirens' long hair wafting on the waves. I closed my eyes and gloried in the motion, the romantic music, the softness of my gown as it wrapped around my body and then unwound to float gracefully in the crystal-clear waters.

"This is the day you have long awaited, Kamoana. We dance together at last!" Startled, I returned to reality to see Prince Pike's amber eyes gaze at me, unblinking.

"Indeed, we do." Smiling until my face hurt, I struggled to think of something innocuous to talk about. "My sister Talulah is singing with the siren choir—did you see her? Hard to miss that silvery-white hair of hers. My sisters all brought food, and I hear there will be entrees from around the world, even the arctic pole! The ice sirens will bring frozen foods, I'd guess." I chuckled at my own joke. Pike probably didn't get it.

"Did you prepare food?" he asked. "I should have sent word of my favorite foods so you could surprise me."

"I didn't make anything; I'm a terrible chef. Mother sent exotic things to eat. Sadly, she couldn't come—there was some sort of unrest back in our home ocean."

"I am disappointed in her absence. I hope to make an important announcement this very evening." His round eyes and sharply chiseled features managed to suggest passion and devotion; how, I don't know. Most mermen maintain a permanent blank expression, which is unsurprising, since they are fishlike from the waist up, just as mermaids are fishlike from the waist down.

I glanced upward. "Those lamps are amazing. They look like bubbles rising."

Glass balls and bottles filled with bioluminescent plankton floated above us, held in place by long strands of seaweed.

"Your mother provided most of the illumination," Prince Pike said, "talented siren that she is. Though one must wonder why a *sahira* and queen would lower herself to such trivialities."

It was midday, but Kranakoa, the sunken city chosen as the site of this year's ball, was so deep in the sea that sunlight couldn't reach it. The glass lamps alone couldn't account for the ballroom's brightness; a subtle but consistent magical glow provided the roofless chamber with romantic atmosphere.

"Because she enjoys it," I answered lightly. But that wasn't the only reason. Queen Pukai, the most powerful *sahira* ever seen among merfolk, was deeply romantic at heart. After losing three husbands, one after another, to tragic deaths—my father most recently—Mother gave up on romance for herself and started seeking it for her daughters. All four of us princesses had been more-or-less promised to aspiring suitors during our childhood, yet

Mother sincerely wished we might marry for love. Her solution? To transform our political matches into love matches, one way or another.

Up to now she had stopped short of using direct magic . . . but then, my sisters had been easily persuaded to love their intended mates and were now happily married. I was the problem child. Mother's patience was wearing thin.

Not until this year had I agreed to attend the annual Siren Song Ball, highlight of the social season, and then only after she mentioned the venue. "Kranakoa? A sunken city sounds so romantic"—I had made an effort to gush a little—"and I've always wished to see the Begaian Sea!"

I'd said nothing about the famous university located on the sea's southern coast near the sunken city, much less the young human who might still be studying or working there.

Although she must have wondered at my sudden enthusiasm, Mother had created for me a costume so amazing that I kept intercepting envious glances from other mermaids. They were all beautiful, being sirens, and many of them wore lovely wraps or pretty shells, but I fluttered among them like a colorful nudibranch or a graceful manta ray.

In place of my usual fabric wrap, I wore gilded scallop shells trimmed in pearls, and from my nearly invisible shoulder straps wafted veils of iridescent fabric that shimmered in the light and draped longer than my tail. My big sister Talulah had loosely braided my black hair with strands of pearls and paua-shell beads that brought out the deep blue of my tail.

Pike danced well, moving his legs much as a human would but with better effect underwater since his large feet were webbed. As the song ended, he twirled me, then tried to draw me close, but I followed the twirl with a few experimental dance moves that made him move back to avoid being swathed in veils. He watched me, his expression intent.

Another merman approached, evidently intending to request my next dance, but Pike gave him a look. As if caught in a riptide, the fellow switched his focus to a different siren.

"The décor is not what captures my interest and heart tonight," Pike said, continuing our conversation as though we'd been talking all along. Although his features resembled those of the intimidating predatory fish for which he'd been named, he managed to give me an adoring gaze.

"I know exactly what you mean," I gushed. "The singing is also sensational. I don't believe the last tune was original to sirens, though. I'm sure I've heard that melody drift out over Faraway Lake from the castle while humans are dancing. It is lovely."

"The song is 'The Blue Daiune,' named for a river not far from your home," he said. "Would humans name a song after a body of water?"

"Oh, yes! Humans spend much of their time on, in, and around water." I was careful to keep my tone both animated and respectful. "If they didn't, how could we sirens ply our trade?"

"You can forget luring humans, for your charms have snared for you the affections of a prince. Yes, Kamoana, your prayers are answered: You are the reason I have anticipated this event. The reason I dance tonight is to finally hold you in my arms where you belong."

"How kind of you to say so, Prince Pike."

He wasn't happy with that response, but he could hardly object. As the siren choir began singing the next dance tune, we twirled hand in hand above the sandy ballroom floor, my tail wafting smoothly, his webbed feet kicking in perfect rhythm. Other couples moved around us. The vividly colored hair and tails of the sirens and the mermen's glistening scales gave the scene vibrant beauty.

Prince Pike's coloring was in the muted hues typical of a freshwater merman, a dark green with pale yellow spots over most of his body, and his webbed arms, hands, and feet were brown. He was considered extraordinarily handsome in freshwater circles. Around us swam many mermen from tropical seas who flaunted brilliant colors and extra fins, some of them rather stunning. Nevertheless, they were no threat to Pike's hopes. My interest focused in an entirely different direction.

So far, I'd found no opportunity to pursue that interest. For two hours I'd been thwarting Pike's attempts at romantic talk and a marriage proposal. Every time I accepted a dance with another merman, Pike waited on the outskirts, watching with such an intimidating stare that my unlucky partner could hardly concentrate. The prince was a terrible flirt, but he was determined to have me—undoubtedly for the political connection our marriage would ensure him—and he seemed unable to conceive of my not wishing to marry him. Crown Prince Pike of Onterrica was considered the hottest match on the marriage market. Throughout the ball I'd been intercepting envious glares from other mermaids. But he had always left me cold, even before I gave my heart away to a most inappropriate person, to a boy my mother would never accept as her son-in-law.

Hope of seeing that boy again was the reason I had come to this year's Siren Song Ball.

As the music ended and Pike twirled me one last time, I smiled at him and said, "Whew! That's enough dancing for me for a while. I need to slip away for a few minutes. Why don't you ask Mellisant to dance the next one with you?"

The golden-haired siren had been watching us all evening with mournful green eyes.

"But I don't wish to dance with anyone but you," Pike said. Most mermen speak in a near-monotone and have expressionless faces, but Pike's voice reverberated with frustration, and his piscine features emoted passion. The merprince had a decided flair for acting.

"And Mellisant wishes to dance with no one but you, poor girl. Do it for my sake," I said with another smile. My smile muscles ached after all their insincere work, but I wished to keep Pike happy for the present.

Before he could answer, a rumble made everyone look up. "Is that an earthquake?" a quivering voice inquired.

"Oh no!" a siren cried. "We should swim away from all these rocks!"

There was a flicker of light that turned our surroundings green, and a soundwave travelled through the water to shiver our skin and scales.

"Never fear. It is only a thunderstorm, and a storm at the surface should not endanger us here, unless a ship sinks down onto the sea floor," Bream, one of my brothers-in-law, said, holding out his webbed hands and arms in a calming gesture. "Talk about crashing a party." As usual, his attempt at humor fell flat.

While merfolk milled around, talking and gazing apprehensively toward the distant surface, I took the opportunity to slip behind a crumbled wall and then swim away from the ballroom, away from the shore, at top speed, keeping close to the sea floor. A few guards had been posted, but they paid no attention to merfolk leaving the ball, only to those trying to enter. Once out of sight, I switched direction and swam west. I knew the general direction of the university on the shore of Barbacha, but I needed help.

"Nelumbo!" I called, my siren voice ringing through the water. I counted on noise at the ball to keep anyone there from hearing me. "Nelumbo, where are you?" He had accompanied me through the water door early that morning, so I knew he must be near.

Soon, glowing yellow eyes loomed in the water. Light couldn't penetrate this deep into the sea, but I could hardly mistake the great serpent's huge, weedy-looking head.

"There you are! I thought I would never get out of that place. I've been trying to escape for hours, and now I'm afraid Pike will notify Mother that I'm missing. Do you know where Tor is? Can you take me to him? We must hurry!"

Surface storms seldom affected my life significantly, so I didn't consider the possibly of the thunderstorm interfering with my plans.

Nelumbo presented me with the back of his head. I grabbed hold of two of his large spikes and braced my tail between two others. "Ready," I called out.

Nelumbo took off, slithering through the water at such speed that I had to hide my face against his scaly neck while my filmy gown billowed behind me. He gradually rose toward the surface, and I wondered if we were approaching land.

Through the water I heard a thrumming noise, then we popped above the surface and I drew a breath that seemed to be half air and half water. Confused, I blinked at our surroundings and realized that rain pounded on my head. Right. The storm. Waves rose around us, reminding me of the mountains surrounding my lake home.

Lightning flashed directly overhead, and a crack of thunder numbed my ears. We were in deadly danger here on the surface during a lightning storm. But just ahead I saw something that brought my heart to my throat: a large boat lying on its side and bobbing clumsily in the waves. Its engine still labored on, making that thrumming noise I'd heard. "It's sinking!" I shouted. "Where are the humans?"

Nelumbo dove underwater again—I nearly lost my hold on him—and surfaced before I quite drew a breath. Just ahead, a lifeboat bobbed in the water. I jumped off Nelumbo's neck, reached the boat in two swipes of my tail, caught hold of its gunwale, and pulled myself up to look inside. Two people sat on its seats, coughing and moaning. One was a woman. The other appeared to be male, but he wasn't Tor.

I dropped back underwater. "Was Tor on the boat?" I asked.

Nelumbo's head bobbed up and down. "We've got to find him!" I shouted. We split up and began combing the area. A life ring bobbed on the waves, empty. A keg floated past me. He wouldn't be able to climb on top of that anyway. I barely restrained my panic. "Tor! Where are you, Tor?" I threw my siren voice into the wind and under the water.

An answer drifted to my ears: "Here."

"Nelumbo!" I called underwater. "He's over here somewhere."

I swam in what I hoped was the right direction. "Tor, call again!"

"Help! Somebody help me!"

I homed in on that voice. "I'm coming. Hold on."

I saw a piece of something in a valley between waves—a sail? A tarp? It was tangled in ropes and attached to floats. A man clung to the floating mess, but whatever place he caught hold of sank beneath him, so he was obliged to keep moving around the edges. I couldn't recognize him as Tor, yet I swam up behind him and caught him around the waist and chest. The man's body tensed, and I felt his terror radiate through me. "I've got you. You'll be safe now."

A wave smacked over us as if to mock me. The man was lean but heavy, and his violent flailing made him harder to rescue. After that wave passed, the tangled raft was gone. The man sputtered and coughed, his chest heaving in my grasp. "I'm so sorry," I said. "Are you . . . are you Tor?"

He sucked in a ragged breath and went still. I felt him shaking as his hands pressed over mine. "K-Kammy?"

10

HE REMEMBERED ME! How could this be? My mother had stolen his memories of me six years ago!

"Yes, I'm here, Tor!"

What if I hadn't been here? He would have drowned! The realization renewed my panic, and I burst into tears. My tail worked hard to keep his head above water, but the rest of me simply clung to him, my face pressed into the hood of his sopping jacket.

"I hear you and feel you, but I can't see you. Am I dreaming?" His voice was hoarse, and he gasped for breath. There was blood on his head, diluted by rain and the wash of waves.

"No, this is all too real, Tor. What happened?" I knew he would do better if I could keep him awake and talking. The water felt warm to me, but I could feel him shivering. I ducked my face underwater and called my sea serpent again.

When I surfaced, Tor was shaking his head. "The others. My colleagues. Where are they?" Dread weighted his voice.

"Two people are in a lifeboat. Nelumbo will push them to safety. How many people were on the big boat? Oh wait! Here comes the lifeboat now." It came skimming over the waves with purpose, and I saw coils of my serpent following along behind it. Should I try to boost Tor into the boat? Nelumbo could push the boat more efficiently than I could haul Tor along with me.

"Four," Tor said, then repeated it. "Four of us."

Someone was missing? Horror gripped me again until I looked to the boat . . . and counted three heads. "They're all here, Tor. Your friends are safe. Nelumbo rescued them, all three."

"Nelumbo. The lake monster," he mumbled.

"That's right, but he's here in the sea now." I spoke into Tor's ear, keeping my voice calm and reassuring, "I'm going to help you into the boat with your friends, and Nelumbo will push you back to shore and safety." Strong hands suddenly clutched my wrists, and he tried to turn to face me, but I turned with him.

"No! Kammy, don't leave me! If you leave, I might forget you again. I can't lose you." He was babbling, half sobbing, and sounded so desperate that I didn't have the heart to argue. The poor boy had nearly drowned.

"I will swim right alongside and be there when you reach the shore."

Another wave broke over us. This time I focused on keeping his head above water. He coughed, shaking his head and mumbling, "Don't let go. I'll wake up and you'll be gone."

"I don't think I could haul you all the way back to shore in this storm, and you're in no condition to do our usual method anyway." I looked at Nelumbo. His yellow eyes expressed no opinion. The three people in the boat hadn't yet noticed us. They bailed water with their hands, their eyes wide and terrified. Whether they feared the storm or Nelumbo more, I couldn't be sure. They could all see the serpent, but none of them could see me, and they hadn't yet noticed Tor.

"I remember. I remember how you hauled me around," Tor murmured. "I remember your voice. Oh Kammy, I want to see your face, but I'm afraid . . ." His voice trailed off and his head dropped forward.

"No, don't fall asleep. You need to stay awake, Tor!" I spun him around to face me, pumping with my tail to keep us on top of the waves. Another one broke over our heads anyway, and Tor spluttered and flailed, coughing, his hands reaching for me. He couldn't drown me, but I was afraid he would exhaust himself and pass out.

I caught his wrist, pulled him toward me, and wrapped my arms around his body beneath his arms until our faces nearly touched. I felt his tension melt away as I said fiercely, "I won't let you drown. I've finally found you after all these years, and I'm not going to let you die."

His hands lightly touched my shoulders, my hair, and my face. "You're real? No, I'll wake up and it will all be a dream again."

Blood-tinged water dripped from his thick eyebrows and lashes. I glimpsed a shallow cut at his hair line; it didn't look dangerous. His eyes were the same, but a beard? How strange it looked to me! Yet I didn't care. He was Tor. "I could climb into the boat with you," I offered. "Would that be better?"

He merely stared at me, too confused to answer, so I made the decision for him. While Nelumbo held the boat steady, I boosted my friend over its side. He landed with a splash and a grunt, and the others first swore at him, then greeted him with joy. "We thought you'd drowned!" one of them cried. "Now help us bail!"

Ignoring them, Tor hung his head over the side. "Kammy!" he shouted.

"I'm here. Balance the boat, and I'll jump in."

He sat back and braced himself. With a determined flick of my tail, I popped out of the water and landed hard, my side connecting with a flat seat. "Ouch!"

Just as I sat up, the boat began to move rapidly, and my shoulder hit someone's knee. "Excuse me!" I gasped.

As soon as I spoke, the young man saw me, and his face went slack. "Wh-where did you come from?" Swearing in falsetto, he scrambled over the next seat and into the stern, where he sat down, gripped the seat with both hands, and stared at me, open-mouthed.

It stopped raining, and the clouds parted. Brilliant sunlight fell on us, and everyone blinked in the glare as the boat bobbed upon those wild waves.

"What's wrong with you, Jonathan? What are you staring at?" It was a woman's voice.

"Good afternoon, madam," I said in her direction. "Please pardon my intrusion."

Her face went slack, and she swore in surprise, ending with "It's a mermaid!"

"Aunt Saliha, are you hallucinating?" asked a voice from the bow of the boat, behind me.

"No, she really can see me," I answered, turning. "And now so can you."

A young woman met my gaze, blinking hard, and sat bolt upright. "A siren!" She shifted her stare to her aunt. "Your dream came true, Auntie! She's a real siren!"

"Or else we're all enchanted," the young man said, his voice shaking. "I feel strange when I look at you, siren. I've never seen anything so beautiful! Are you going to eat us?"

"You're siren-enthralled, Jonathan!" the aunt cried, then turned a fiery glare on me. "Get away from us, fey creature!"

At this, Tor seemed to wake up. "Stop being superstitious and show some gratitude," he said. "Kamoana and Nelumbo are rescuing us." While he was speaking, he pulled off his wet jacket and wrapped it around me. He then scooped me up and helped me sit upright on the seat beside him, keeping one arm around my shoulders in a protective position. I felt grateful for the jacket and now understood why Mother warned her daughters so frequently that humans might react to the sight of us in alarming ways.

Secure in Tor's grasp, I again addressed the young man Jonathan. "Furthermore, it's been centuries since sirens ate humans. We're civilized now."

"These are my colleagues," Tor told me. "I apologize for their bad manners." He still looked dazed and pale, yet I saw deep concern for me in his face. Turning to the others, he spoke in a tone that made me sit straighter and feel warm inside. "This lady siren is my friend Kamoana. We met years ago when she rescued me from a turul." He looked down at me with wonder in his eyes and seemed to forget our audience, speaking so that only I could hear. "We exchanged letters for a year afterward with Nelumbo's help. Then we were discovered. But now I have found you again."

"What?" Jonathan blurted. "Did you say you've met this siren before?"

The sun ducked behind another cloud, and I felt Tor shiver in the wind. He should be wearing his jacket. But I didn't dare remove it.

"Did you enchant Nora while she was driving? Were you and that monster trying to sink us?" the aunt asked me sharply, in no way convinced by Tor's attempted introduction.

"No, Aunt Saliha," Nora answered for me, "I wasn't enchanted. You know we shouldn't have stayed out so long with that storm coming. And in case you all haven't noticed," she added, "we're moving rapidly toward shore. The monster is pushing us. A good thing, since this lifeboat had neither oars nor flotation devices nor anything else useful." Frustration laced her voice. "We would all be dead by now."

"The bow is riding low in the water," Jonathan said. "I suggest we stop jawing and bail."

They all scrambled into action. Cupping my hands, I followed their example and tossed water overboard. Even though the wind blew much of it back into our faces, we could at least keep pace with the waves attempting to fill the boat. Tor's big hands held twice as much water as mine, but I moved faster. He kept pausing either to rub his head or to stare at me. I saw his gaze take in my braided hair, which was still neat, and my tail, which I tried to keep tucked to one side. His jacket covered most of the rest of me. His gaze was so filled with honest admiration and joy that I couldn't feel uncomfortable. I found myself staring back.

But before I could interpret what I saw in his eyes, Aunt Saliha gave a shout: "Land!" I turned to see a shoreline in the distance, cliffs with white buildings gleaming in sunlight. The storm had mostly passed, though the white-capped waves remained a threat.

"And look, a rescue boat, finally!" Nora staggered upright in the bow, waving both arms. There it was, a shining white craft upon the green hills of water.

I decided to make myself useful. "Cover your ears," I suggested, then called toward the other boat, using projection but no allure: "Help us! Look to your right." To the satisfaction of all, the boat wheeled about and headed toward us. It was a high-powered craft, I could tell by the engine's roar, and equal to facing the remains of this storm.

Three of the castaways focused on their approaching rescuers, but Tor still had eyes only for me. His dilated pupils worried me. A blow to the head must have caused that cut. "Tor, humans are coming to rescue you. I must go now," I told him. "Please come and find me when you can."

"Kammy!" He reached for my arms, but I slipped through his grasp and dived overboard, leaving his jacket in his hands. "No!" I heard him shout, and then a great splash, and when I looked up, there he was, back in the sea, his eyes staring around underwater, wide and frantic. He saw me, and bubbles burst from his mouth.

I should have known he would try to follow me. Quickly I shoved him to the surface. As soon as I held him, he stopped thrashing and clung to the arm I'd wrapped over his shoulder and chest from behind. A flotation device on a rope hit the water nearby, and I dragged Tor to it. "Don't leave me, Kammy," he begged. "Please don't leave me!"

My heart ached, but I dared not listen to his pleas. "I can't come on land, and you need medical help." Once I'd fastened the strange device around him, I turned his face until his glassy eyes met mine. "Tor, after you've recovered your strength, come and find me at Faraway Castle. Please! I'll be waiting."

Submerging, I watched his rescue from below. They hoisted him into the boat first, then his three companions.

I could only hope and pray that he would be all right, and that he would still remember me when he recovered from this trauma.

Nelumbo slipped up behind me and gave my head a nudge. I turned, feeling heavy and sad inside. Certainly in no mood for a party, much less for Pike's company.

"I suppose we'd better head back now."

Nelumbo gave me a sympathetic look—or so I interpreted his deadpan stare—before I climbed back on his neck, and off we went.

I heard singing as we approached Kranakoa, and my heart gave a twinge. What could I do or say to explain my absence? Nothing. Nothing I said would satisfy Pike or my mother.

"Nelumbo, please take me to the door. I've had all the excitement I can handle in one day."

He obediently headed for the water door not far from the sunken city, a shimmering circle suspended in the sea—a portal to any body of water in the world. "Faraway Lake," I said firmly, and swam through. Nelumbo followed me home. I didn't immediately head to the island but swam toward the castle, watching sailboats and kayaks pass overhead. It was a beautiful late-spring afternoon, heading toward evening, and resort guests took full advantage of the warm, clear weather.

I surfaced and bobbed on the gentle waves, clad in my elegant getup. Faraway Castle looked peaceful and dignified seated there amid the mountains, its foot dabbling in the lake's cold water.

Memories flooded over me—memories of bright summer days, of rescue, arguments, and a developing friendship. Heavenly days of swimming with my best friend, showing him my world, and hearing about his. Then reading his letters over the winter and anticipating his return. And oh, our reunion that next summer! Tears trickled down my already wet face.

Would Tor come?

11

MY EYES POPPED open. I sat upright and stared wildly about in confusion. Where was I? The ceiling above, blue sky through tall windows, a soft bed . . . human legs on the bed, attached to my torso . . . I was human. In my room in Faraway Castle.

My heart still raced, but sanity slowly returned. A dream. It was all a dream. But so vivid! So terrifying and . . .

The shipwreck Nora told me about. I really had been there. Nelumbo rescued the others, but Tor . . . I rescued Tor.

I grabbed my cheeks and rubbed hard to shake myself fully awake, breathing in ragged gasps and wiping tears from my face. I truly had loved Tor, with a love so powerful that my heart still hurt from that dream.

There was a sharp knocking sound, and I jerked. What was it?

Then Beatrice asked, "Kamoana, are you ready for dinner?"

Dinner? I couldn't possibly eat! But Tor would be there. But . . . he wouldn't know me. How could I bear it?

I opened my mouth to send the girls away, but a sickening loneliness rolled over me. Instead, I scrambled off the bed, tripped and nearly fell, then blundered my way to the door and opened it.

Fresh and pretty in sundresses, Eddi and Beatrice stared at me, their eyes widening. "What happened to you?" Eddi blurted.

"I fell asleep. Could you wait a moment while I change?"

Beatrice gave Eddi a warning glance. "Of course."

I still wore my swimsuit and coverup. "Do I have a dress like yours?" I asked.

As I had hoped, Beatrice took charge. "We'll pick out your clothes while you go splash your face with cold water and brush out your hair," she said in a tone so motherly that my heartache eased a little.

While I struggled to make myself presentable, my friends whisked through my wardrobe and selected a halter-top sundress, white with orange, yellow, and turquoise swirls and a pattern of palm trees. I considered it gaudy until I tried it on. "You look amazing," Eddi grumbled when I emerged from the bathroom. "We should pick out something ugly for her to wear, Beatrice. Mike will never notice me when she's nearby."

"She's a siren. Clothing doesn't matter," Beatrice reminded her, sounding sympathetic yet flashing me an amused grin. "Mike is too old for you anyway." She closed and locked my door behind us, handed me the key, and we headed for the stairs again. I wanted to request the elevator, that floating room, but it didn't really matter. I could handle the stairs.

Eddi huffed. "I want Mike to take me to the Summer Ball, but he'll probably ask Kamoana. Or that awful Lady Raquel."

I glanced at Eddi's pencil-slim figure and baby-soft features but said nothing. She was a child still, and the men knew it. "Why not see if Kai would take you?" I asked.

"Kai is staff. He can't go to the ball. And he's just a friend anyway." Eddi skimmed down the stairs ahead of us. Beatrice was kind enough to match my slower pace.

"Why is she so worried about men and boys?" I asked when the girl was out of earshot. "She's so young!"

"I expect she wants to marry and escape her father's domination, but it wouldn't work," Beatrice replied, her brow knitting. "He is king of Bilbao, and she is his only heir. He allows her to come to Faraway Castle every summer, hoping she will attract a wealthy prince consort. His country is small and struggling, so Eddi must marry money."

"Do you think that's why she pursues Mike?"

Beatrice smiled and shook her head. "Princess Edurne pursues a new prince or lord every few days. This crush won't last." She gave me a wary glance. "Are you all right, Kamoana? You seem upset."

I shook my head. "I took a nap and had a bad dream." Memories rolled back over me, flashes of Tor's face amid the storm, a face alive with passion, hope, fear, and longing. How could I face him again only to see cold disinterest or outright scorn in his eyes?

Looking unconvinced, Beatrice opened her mouth to pursue the matter, but Eddi rejoined us at the foot of the last staircase. As we crossed the lobby and headed toward the dining room, I felt my legs quivering beneath me. I could scarcely draw a full breath.

"Relax, Kamoana," Eddi said. "You're a siren. What do you have to be nervous about?"

She was right, I thought. Tor had fallen in love with me once. What could stop him from loving me again? As we stepped through the door, I squared my shoulders and lifted my chin.

Nora beckoned as we entered, but I had already zeroed in on Tor, and my legs again felt as steady as sandworms. The university crew had claimed one of the eight-person tables for us. Tor did not so much as look in my direction, and pain shot through my heart.

To my relief, Mike was already seated between Nora and Dr. Benyamina. The men rose as we approached—Mike rather tardily—and held our chairs. The doctor gave me a quick, cool appraisal. "Good evening, ladies," she said. "I hear we may have the pleasure of your company for a snorkeling excursion tomorrow morning. Prince Mike has already agreed to join us."

"We're honored to be asked, but Princess Edurne and I have plans," Beatrice answered as Jonathan seated her. She looked over at me with concern in her eyes and quietly said, "I'm so sorry, I forgot to tell you that Eddi was invited on a cross-country ride."

"You'll be happy enough, Kamoana, since I'll be snorkeling with you," Mike assured me as Tor held my chair. I was too aware of the man behind me to think of an answer for Mike, but Nora drew him into conversation, so it didn't matter.

I thought Tor might sit beside me, but Jonathan slid into the empty seat before I was quite settled. "You look amazing," he said.

I glanced up from arranging a serviette on my lap and found his face closer than I had expected. "Thanks."

I watched Tor move around the table to sit across from Jonathan. For once, he wasn't wearing sunglasses. He glanced at me, and our eyes locked. An eternity passed before someone spoke to him and he turned away.

I dropped my gaze to the table before me and sat perfectly still, trying to quiet my heart, trying to guess his thoughts. His expression had been questioning. Not angry, as I had feared. More . . . curious. Did he remember anything at all?

Dinner was difficult to eat, but I learned to use a fork and knife reasonably well. Jonathan kept offering advice, which I did not appreciate, since it drew attention to my ineptitude. And no matter how polite he was now, I couldn't forget the way he'd stared at me in my dream. Dimples notwithstanding, I would rather dissolve into sea foam than trust a man like him with any part of my future.

"Kamoana," Mike said during a brief lull in the conversation, "I've been invited to the Summer Ball by five different girls today. You'd better stop delaying and make your bid." His smile revealed not a hint of self-doubt.

"You'd better make up your mind and accept the best offer," I replied, and met Nora's gaze with a smile. She gave me a frustrated little grimace.

"I would do so gladly, but you haven't asked me yet." His deep voice held genuine surprise at my lack of perception.

"True." I happened to catch Tor's gaze, but he immediately looked away.

Bless Nora, she distracted the prince again, and after that uncomfortable meal ended, we all headed down to the shore for the beach-volleyball tournament. Ahead of me, Mike, decently clad for once in jeans and a long-sleeved shirt, had Nora on one arm and Eddi on the other, and for the moment, Eddi dominated the conversation, talking about the volleyball players. I caught only the tail end of her lecture: ". . . Lord Ludovic of Grimmelshausen is the best spiker around, Lord Carevo plays in volleyball tournaments all over the continent, and Prince Maximilian is one of the best in the world. Of course, here they all play just for fun."

I had to stifle a laugh, imagining Mike's disgust at hearing this praise of other men. "I'm the best swimmer in my kingdom," he said when Eddi paused for breath. "No one else can—"

"Lord Ludovic plays water polo too, so you know he's an amazing swimmer," Eddi continued her spiel. Mike was motivated, but Eddi had the faster tongue.

"Tomorrow you'll see me swim," Mike told Nora. "I'm not at my best, of course, but I venture to guess that no one will equal my speed and power."

Nora chuckled. "When are you ever at your best, Mike? Perhaps you have never quite achieved it yet." When he floundered for an answer, she offered him an easier question. "Has anyone ever been your equal? Or if anyone ever gives you a real challenge, do you conveniently forget?"

The laughter in her voice amused me, but Mike seemed deaf to it. People like him, assured of their own perfection and desirability, never did recognize sarcasm when they heard it. I knew one or two mermen with that problem.

"I'll race you tomorrow, if you like," Nora offered with her usual good humor. "Just so I can observe your amazing speed as I fall behind, of course."

They soon outpaced us, but I thought I heard Mike accept her offer.

"I can hardly wait to watch that race," Jonathan said with heavy sarcasm. "Nora's a strong swimmer but not fast." He walked beside me along the path. "Are you warm enough? You should have brought a wrap. Tell me if you get cold, and I'll put my arm around you."

I didn't grace that offer with a response.

When we finally reached the beach, I delayed choosing a chair, hoping to find a way to avoid sitting beside him. When Mike and Nora invited me and Beatrice to sit with them, I took the chair next to Mike's. Beatrice sat on my right, and the others settled somewhere behind us. Eddi returned from talking with friends and gave me an accusing look. "I wanted to sit beside Mike."

"I have only two sides," he said with true sympathy, "and there are so many women."

Nora and I both burst into giggles. Mike looked back and forth between us, his muscled arms draped over the chair arms, his long legs sprawled out on the sand. "What do you two find amusing?" he asked, sounding indulgent. "I was talking to Princess Eddi and missed it."

That comment set us both off again. Nora patted his arm and said, "Mike, you are the most entertaining guy I have ever met. There is never a dull conversation with you around."

"And you are a most perceptive woman, Nora Rachid." He laid his hand over hers on his arm, nodding his appreciation.

Before the games began, the chair arrangement had altered until we were all in a sort of semicircle facing the sandy court, with other people crowding in. Eddi entertained us with her knowledge of the sport, informing us when the various lords and princes made certain plays.

The volleyball players leaped and dove after the ball, whacking it into the air and over the net. Just as I began to guess at the rules, the match was over. Two teams of girls took over the court next. They were also amazingly strong and nimble.

As the sun slipped behind the mountains, the air chilled, driving guests to gather around campfires. Strings of twinkling lights chased away shadows. Music played, and some people danced on the sand. Dr. Benyamina had excused herself some time ago, looking angry about something. Beatrice and Eddi stood talking with other friends. Somewhere behind us, Mike entertained Nora with tales about ice skating with bare feet. I sat on the sun-warmed sand between Tor and Jonathan, watching another two teams play volleyball under the artificial lights. Jonathan kept trying to draw me into conversation, but I pretended to focus on the game.

I was hyperaware of Tor's presence beside me. He sat with his knees up, hands propped behind him. Because of my dress, I had to sit with my legs tucked to one side, a familiar position. I sat with my feet toward Jonathan and leaned on one hand. My hair spilled over my shoulder to drag on the sand. I think it sometimes brushed Tor's arm.

Here I was, near enough to touch him yet unable to talk with him beyond a question or two about the rules of volleyball. He seemed to follow the action, but I thought he might be as aware of me as I was of him. As frustrated? I couldn't be sure.

Then a girl hit a ball so hard and wildly that it rocketed straight toward us. Before I could even throw my hands up, Tor caught the ball with his left hand directly in front of my face. I turned to stare at him, and he asked, "Are you all right?" With a flick of his wrist, he tossed the ball back into play.

"Yes, thanks to you."

He nearly smiled. I turned my head just as he put his hand back, right through my hair. "Uh, sorry," he said, and cleared his throat. I smiled at him over my shoulder, and he left his hand there under my hair.

"That was a nice catch," Jonathan said grudgingly. "Why aren't you playing, Tor?"

"You know I'm no good at sports."

Jonathan mumbled something I didn't catch, because at that moment a young man seemed to appear from nowhere and crouched before Tor. He had brown skin, black hair, and large dark eyes.

"Your Highness," Tor greeted him in evident surprise.

"I heard you were back but haven't seen you around." The prince's voice held unspoken accusation. "Are you recovered?"

"I'm fine, Omar. I hear I owe you an apology."

"You *hear*? Don't you know it? I might have drowned!" He sounded irritated.

I felt Tor's tension, but he didn't look my way. "Uh, can we talk somewhere else?" He scrambled to his feet, blocking the prince from my sight, and the two men walked away.

Jonathan turned to me with a grin. "At last. I thought he would never take the hint and leave. It's going to be a beautiful moonlit evening. Would you like to take a walk?"

Before I could answer, Eddi dropped on her knees in Tor's place, rubbing her bare arms. "Kamoana, that guy Tor asked me to walk back with you. Beatrice and I are ready if you are. I'm freezing!"

"Me, too," I answered, probably sounding a little too eager, and scrambled to my feet. "Thanks for the offer, Jonathan, but I'm ready to go inside. Tomorrow's going to be busy!"

12

MY EYELIDS FELT glued shut, but it was morning, and someone was knocking at my door. I struggled to sit upright, then dropped my face into my hands. The brownie who cleaned my room and brought fresh towels had long since come and gone. The sun was up, and if I wanted to eat before our outing, I needed to move. "Hello?" My voice cracked.

"Kamoana, are you coming to breakfast?" Beatrice asked, trying to keep her voice hushed.

I rubbed my eyes. "Go on without me," I called. "I'll be down soon."

"Are you sure?"

"I'm sure."

"If we don't see you, have fun today."

"Thanks." Rubbing my eyes didn't help. They burned like I'd scrubbed sand into them. So many dreams, all night long! I might have swum laps across the Begaian Sea during the night, so aching and exhausted was my body. It would take hours to process those dreams if I could even remember them all.

The pine tree we'd passed in the boat yesterday? My dreams revealed that I'd first seen Tor under that tree, a crazy birdwatcher trying to hide from a hungry turul. I had rescued him, though we both nearly died more than once that day.

Tor wore glasses back then. Glasses with clear lenses. He'd told me he was nearsighted, a concept I still didn't understand. But when he used a swim mask, he'd worn lenses he could put directly on his eyes. He must use those all the time now.

Now I remembered Tor as a boy in a wetsuit—tall and much skinnier than now, with a mop of sun-bleached hair on top and a rare but sweet grin.

So many wonderful little memories of jokes, laughter, competition, arguments.

I had written letters, entrusting them to Nelumbo to deliver to Tor's school, and received precious letters back. I frowned and rubbed my face. What had become of those letters? I could only hope Mother hadn't destroyed them.

Tor returned to Faraway Castle the following summer. We'd had one beautiful day together, a day filled with a strange new awareness brought by the passage of time and our ever-deepening affection for each other. My first kiss.

My mother found us the second day, and the happy dreams twisted into nightmares. Mother stole Tor's memory and forbade me to speak to him again. I took him back to our cove, heart-broken by his blank stare and silence. But just before he climbed ashore, I stole a kiss. So quick—his lips cold and unresponsive. Yet I'd glimpsed a flicker of something in his eyes before I swam away.

Six long years had passed since the day my mother stole Tor from me. I was no longer a sixteen-year-old merchild. Mother had no right to manipulate me with spells and try to decide my future. Yet who could stop her?

I wasn't sure I could bear to face Tor again after those dreams. Yesterday provided moments of connection—I hoped—but today he might regard me with the unconcern of a stranger. Then again, on the lake he almost always wore sunglasses, so I couldn't read his expression anyway. Last night, when I caught glimpses of his eyes, they were just as I remembered from my dreams: cool blue, keen, nearly shrouded by his lashes.

I decided I could handle the pain for another day. With any luck, I might relight a spark of interest. I was almost certain he felt something for me. Even suspicion and resentment were better than apathy.

I dragged myself out of bed and dressed in the clothes I had laid out the night before. A one-piece swimsuit on loan from Beatrice and the fresh towels supplied by the brownie were sufficient for my needs. Over the suit, I wore shorts, a top, a sunhat, and a jacket. At Beatrice's suggestion I brought a bottle of water, which seemed strange to me, but humans didn't drink the lake water. Tor was to collect sack lunches at the dining hall, and I could borrow a wetsuit and snorkeling gear at the docks.

Since the elevator was vacant, I used it. After stopping at every floor, I finally reached the lobby. Maybe pushing all of the buttons hadn't been a bright idea, but I found the ground floor eventually.

"Your group is down at the boat already, Kamoana," said Sten, the dwarf at the front desk, as I rushed for the lobby doors.

"Thanks!" I called back. I pushed open an outer door and hurried across the portico and down the path to the lake. My feet protested, but my legs and back felt better today.

To my relief, the group seemed nowhere near ready to embark. Mike and Tor faced off beside the gear-storage shed. Sunlight glinted off Tor's short hair, and his wetsuit highlighted his long, lean, swimmer's build. Feeling suddenly too warm, I slowed my steps. But then Mike caught sight of me and beckoned me over, his chest and arm muscles flexing. He wore only swim trunks again.

A nearby lifeguard fanned herself and sighed, "Be still, my heart!"

Mike flashed her his perfect smile before returning his focus to me. "Kamoana, I was just telling Tor, here, that no true swimmer requires a rubber suit or a mask, let alone fake fins. If a man cannot swim using the equipment he was given at birth, he should not enter the water."

"Let's see if you feel that way after ten minutes submerged in the lake," Tor said.

"I'm sure Kamoana will agree with me," Mike returned, flashing me a superior smile.

"You found a wetsuit in my size?" I asked Tor.

He handed one over without looking at me, but I thought I saw his lips twitch. "This should fit."

"Thank you." I didn't need to look at Mike to enjoy his dismay. He was still arguing when I entered the tiny changing room and shimmied into the uncomfortable wetsuit. It felt stiff and ugly but fit me well enough.

Just as I picked up my daypack and opened the door, Jonathan walked up the dock, already suited up. "I thought you weren't allowed to use the resort's equipment, Tor."

"I always use my own swim gear," Tor replied over one shoulder while sorting through fins. "Just helping these two get suited up. Nora made reservations for them."

"Ungracious, isn't he?" Mike commented to Jonathan, who rolled his eyes and walked on. Shaking his head, Mike turned to me. "Tor is probably bad-tempered because he's enchanted."

Tor spun toward us, a fin in each hand. "Enchanted? You can sense enchantment on me?"

Mike looked amused. "You positively reek of magic."

My mother's spell, of course. I couldn't sense it myself, but I was under enchantment too, and I've never been skilled at detecting spells. I hadn't even detected that Mike possessed a measure of magic.

Tor dropped the fins. "Am I siren-enthralled?" he asked, his deep voice like a growl.

Mike answered airily, "No, this is a totally different style of magic. More of a suppression—" He suddenly stopped speaking, then blurted, "Not siren enchantment, for sure." His mouth shut tight, and without another word, he hurried to the boat.

Tor glanced around at the lifeguard and waiting guests, then led me to the side of the shed. When I stood within inches of him, he asked in a near whisper, "So, you really haven't enchanted me?"

I shook my head, struggling to hide my hurt feelings. "My sisters enthrall men. I don't. Ever."

He gripped his head with both hands, pulling them down over his beard. "But I'm under a suppression spell? I thought I must be losing my mind. People keep telling me about things I've said and done, and I have no memory of any of it." He gave a mirthless laugh. "One of the lifeguards asked me yesterday afternoon if I was feeling well. According to her, she took me off the siren island a few days ago. I was talking with a siren there." He turned and gave me a direct look. "Was it you?"

"It might have been, but I have no memory of that day."

"Honestly?" He looked skeptical.

To my surprise, I was able to say, "My memories were wiped too, but they've been returning to me in dreams. I don't know why. I remember rescuing you after the shipwreck now. I had no memory of that yesterday morning."

"What else do you remember?"

I just looked at him, but he must have seen something in my eyes. He turned away, blinking behind those sunglasses, and muscles clenched in his jaw. "If not for my obligation to entertain these colleagues, I would leave this resort today. This moment. I'm going crazy . . . and being around you— Why do you have to be so—" He stopped and gave his head a shake.

"So . . . what?" I asked, my fists clenching. "Honest? Vulnerable? Helpless?"

Blood rose into his face, and he couldn't meet my gaze. "Hardly helpless. Look, I promised to make this outing, so here I am." He pulled off his sunglasses and gave me a direct stare. "Do your worst."

Slamming his glasses back on his face, Tor stepped around me, between other guests, and into the shed to retrieve a mask, snorkel, and pair of swim fins, which he handed to me. I walked to the boat by myself in a haze of hurt.

When I approached, Jonathan and Dr. Benyamina were huddled at the end of the dock in a private conference. Nora, in a hot-pink wetsuit, greeted me with her sunny smile.

"Need help untying anything?" I asked.

Giving me a wink and a little head shake, she turned to Mike, who already sprawled in the boat, his arms across the seat back. "I wish I had a strong man to help me untie this boat," she said clearly.

"Why, Nora, you need only to ask," Mike said, and jumped back onto the dock.

No one made me forget troubles like Nora could. Grinning, I threw my gear into the bow and climbed in after it. Someone's gear was already there, taking up much of the small floor space.

Nora was still showing Mike how to untie the first knot when Tor arrived and hopped into the boat.

"I'll start it up," he offered.

Dr. Benyamina instantly turned around. "You're not allowed to touch anything on the boat besides your seat." Climbing aboard, she ordered, "Jonathan, help that idiot prince push us off."

But Mike left the task to Jonathan and Nora, resuming his former seat. "You should come back here and sit with me, Kamoana," he called. "This is your chance to have me all to yourself. We can swim together and look at fish. You like fish, right?"

I could almost smile. "I do like fish. You are kind to offer, Prince Mike, but I'll be just fine up here."

Mike stood up. "I'll come up front with you. Tor was rude to accuse you of siren-calling him. Why would you bother calling him when you already have me?"

"Why, indeed?" I said without looking at Tor.

Engine rumbling, the boat started backing out just as Nora followed Jonathan aboard and gave Mike's chest a shove that dropped him back into his seat. "Make room for Nora, Mr. Too-Gorgeous-to-Be-Real." Plopping down beside him, she batted puppy-dog eyes. "You promised to tell me about the time you wrestled three opponents at once and pinned them all."

"Did I? Well, it truly is an astounding story."

As he launched into another anecdote starring his glorious self, I turned toward the bow, tucked up my feet, set my chin on my folded hands on the gunwale, and shed a few quiet tears. Someone joined me in the bow. Marvelous. It had to be Jonathan or Tor, and I wanted neither.

The boat slowed and shifted out of reverse, the engine's rumble turned to a roar, and we were off. "Kamoana, I need you to direct me," called Dr. Benyamina.

"That way." When I pointed north, she followed my direction. It was Tor seated behind me on the facing seat; I knew without looking around. Jonathan would have been talking by now.

The wind and water chilled me as we gained speed. I had braided my hair, but strands pulled loose and whipped around my face. Eyes down, I scooted backward along the seat to sit just in front of the windshield on the driver's side. "That way," I pointed again. "Slower here."

Dr. Benyamina glared at me. "Our trip is to the island, not a bay."

"The first part of our tour takes us to a quiet bay where goldeneye ducks nest," I said, trying to sound like one of the Faraway Castle guides. Tor might hate me, but I intended to keep my promise.

"What are goldeneye ducks?" Nora called from the back seat. "That sounds like fun."

I glanced at Tor seated across from me, the bill of his cap pulled low over his sunglasses. The corner of his mouth twitched as I answered, "Goldeneye ducks have been rare in this region for many years. Sighting even one duck is a treat. But recently they have returned to Faraway Lake, and several pair nest in this particular back bay."

"I like ducks," Mike said. "They are particularly tasty in the autumn, when wild rice grows along the lake shores at home."

Nora laughed. "We're here to look at these ducks, not eat them, silly. And don't let Tor hear you talk about eating his pet obsessions. You might as well speak of roasting a phoenix."

Mike chuckled heartily. "No one would be so foolish as to roast a bird that is born from its own ashes. Have I ever mentioned the sardine-eating contest I won?"

"Eww," Nora responded. "I have never cared for smoked fish. And the idea of eating their bones!" She grimaced.

"Exactly. Sardines must be swallowed whole, fresh from the ocean, to be at their peak," Mike said. "I have never understood why people would smoke them."

"Another sushi fanatic," Jonathan said, his tone wry.

"My opponents and I each stood before a school of sardines, ready for the signal—"

I tuned out Mike's story as we approached the bay. "Once we pass that point, we'll need to slow down and turn right. Everyone needs to be very quiet. If we're lucky, we might see a hen with her ducklings."

"Oh, I hope we see ducklings!" Nora said.

She was happy a few minutes later. A lovely goldeneye duck with nine newly hatched babies swam almost directly across our path. The doctor stopped the boat, letting it drift forward in idle while the tiny creatures paddled to follow their mother. Even Dr. Benyamina's face softened slightly at the sight. I heard a clicking sound and turned to see Tor hanging over the side, wielding a camera.

Jonathan laughed. "While we're admiring birds, you must hear the story of Tor's obsession with the impossible and invisible.

Along with chasing after ducks, he also hunts down birds that don't exist, like some gigantic eagle from Kablar or Tiszaroff or one of those remote countries thereabouts. He's even told me that he saw one in these mountains when he was a kid."

"If you're referring to the turul, it is an actual bird," Tor said firmly, still snapping photos. A goldeneye drake joined the little family, inspiring more photography.

"I've seen a turul," I said abruptly. "Seven years ago. I think it was planning to nest on resort property, on a pine tree across the lake over there"—I pointed in the general direction—"but the Gamekeeper put a stop to that. Too dangerous for guests and staff. Turuls have been known to prey on humans and merfolk when they have opportunity."

Several pairs of eyes pinned me in place. "You've seen a turul?" Dr. Benyamina said, her voice laden with doubt. "Are you certain it wasn't just a very large eagle?"

"I'm quite certain. It nearly caught me."

A short silence followed. I particularly felt Tor's intent stare. He had stopped clicking photos long enough to study my face.

"Who's the Gamekeeper?" Jonathan asked. "And how could anyone control a bird that big?"

Wishing turuls had never been mentioned, I replied, "The Gamekeeper watches over all magical beings on Faraway Castle property. A few other *sahirae* watch over the resort as well. You can imagine that with so many important humans assembling here, it could easily be a tempting target for malevolent beings of all varieties."

"Tor is finished taking photos, and the ducks are gone. Let's go," Jonathan said abruptly.

Dr. Benyamina nodded and turned the boat around. Tor settled back in his seat, caught my eye, and nodded with a little smile. The ducks were a hit. One point for me.

13

A S WE WHISKED across the lake's smooth surface toward Palau Kalah, Nora called to me, "Tell us more about the island. Is it really tropical? How did it get here?"

Her eyes were wide and interested. I couldn't help smiling as I called back to her: "Yes, it really is tropical. Queen Pukai, the great siren *sahira*, wanted a piece of home, so she moved the island here along with a good chunk of ocean. Somewhere on the other side of the world is a patch of lake water filled with fish from Faraway Lake."

"Are they trapped there?" Nora sounded concerned.

"They don't know they're in the ocean. Fish swim and birds fly from here"—I pointed to the lake beneath us—"to there"—I pointed to the far side of the island—"and never know they were briefly across the world. The same is true of the tropical creatures. They can leave the island and swim out into the South Seas anytime they wish. But sentient beings travel from lake to ocean, or vice versa."

I paused to say, "This would be a good place to stop." The doctor throttled down, and our wake rushed past us. Tor rose and prepared to drop the bow anchor.

"Fascinating!" Nora exulted. "Today I get to snorkel around a tropical island! I've only ever studied fish in cold places before. Are you sure we needed the wetsuits?"

"You'll be far more comfortable," Tor said. "And don't touch anything without asking first. There are poisonous creatures in that part of the world." He lowered the anchor, then headed aft, but Jonathan was already dropping the second anchor.

"What about sharks?" Dr. Benyamina asked.

"We see them occasionally," I answered, "but Nelumbo will join us, I'm sure. No sharks go near him. I'm more concerned about other guests seeing us at the island. I had us park this far away so no one on the running trail will report seeing a boat at the island."

While I sorted out my swim fins and other gear, Tor said, "Nora, would you give these to Kamoana." He handed her something round and whitish.

"Sure!" She quickly traded places with him. "You'll need these. They're socks, to keep your feet from blistering."

"What is blistering?"

"It hurts, and it happens when swim fins rub on your skin." She helped me with my socks, fins, gloves, and mask. "You and Tor have a history, don't you?" she asked quietly.

"Yes, but I think it is only history," I admitted.

She gave me a secretive smile. "I don't. Keep doing whatever you're doing. I've never seen him look at any woman the way he looks at you."

Mike protested noisily from the back of the boat. "I specifically told you not to bring gear for me! I can see why a woman might need such devices, but my feet provide plenty of propulsion, and I do not need to breathe through a tube. That suit would be too tight across the shoulders and restrict my movement." He didn't say the words, but his opinion of men who wore wetsuits and swim fins was evident.

"The suits stretch. You could put it on over your swim trunks," Tor told him, but Mike remained unconvinced.

"No rubber suit for me."

Tor gave Nora a look, but she rolled her eyes and shook her head. "It's his funeral."

I gave her a questioning look.

"It means, he makes his own choices," she explained, "and he reaps the consequences."

I glanced back at Mike, suddenly worried. But no matter what Nora might say, I knew she would make sure nothing bad happened to him, and so would Tor. The man was an idiot, but he was harmless enough.

One by one, we jumped into the lake feet first. It felt strange beyond words to leap into my home world wearing a mask, wetsuit, and fake fins! I found the fins nearly as effective as my tail in keeping me afloat. After Nora instructed Mike how to tread water, we all gathered in a circle, and I pointed out the rock we needed to aim for. When the tide was going in or out, there could be some nasty currents around Palau Kalah, but I knew the places to avoid. My objective was a secluded lagoon on the northwest shore.

Something bumped me from behind. Startled, I turned to stare into a slick gray face with small yellow eyes and long white whiskers framing a mouth as wide as the length of my forearm. "Fathoms!" I cried and wrapped my arms around his thick body.

"You know that fish?" the doctor asked in her deep, serious voice, and the others watched in wonder as my fishy friend writhed with happiness and purred in my arms.

Instead of asking, "Isn't it obvious?" I smiled. "Years ago, when Fathoms was about half this size, I rescued him from some resort guests, young boys who'd sneaked fishing gear into a rowboat and hooked him, right here." I pointed to the tear in the fish's upper lip. "He's been my friend ever since."

"Catfish have such tiny brains, I wouldn't have guessed it had the intelligence to distinguish one person from another," she said. "Interesting."

Her dismissive tone irritated me. "He is quite intelligent. I've taught him several tricks, and he understands much of what I say. He even abstains from eating ducklings because he knows I disapprove."

"Smart enough to abstain when you're around anyway," Jonathan said with a smirk. "That is one of the ugliest fish I've ever seen."

"You should see the sturgeons in my kingdom's lakes," Mike said. "They make this fellow look small and ordinary."

Fathoms gave both men a look even colder than his usual expression. Then he turned back to me and shoved his face under my hand. I gently scratched around his gills and fins.

"We'd better get moving before Mike turns into an icicle," Nora said. "I like your fish, Kamoana, but he looks slimy." Her attention returned to Mike, who was visibly struggling to remain afloat.

When Fathoms approached Tor and started bumping the man's chest with his face and wriggling his fins and body from head to tail, Tor gave me a questioning look.

"You and he were good friends," I said.

I couldn't read Tor's expression, but he stroked the catfish's broad back and rubbed around his tiny dorsal fin. "He really is smart if he remembers that far back. Maybe he saw me earlier this week."

Into the following silence, I heard Mike say, "You needn't worry about me. I have won every swimming race in my kingdom these many years. No one has come close to breaking my records."

"Then I challenge you to a race," Nora said. "First one to that rock Kamoana pointed out wins. Go!" And she took off, swimming with the stroke humans often use, but far faster with her swim fins. Now that I was human, I wasn't quite sure how to swim. But I set out, trying to copy Nora's style.

I had slogged along a short distance before someone tapped my shoulder. I paused, using my fins to balance upright.

Tor put his mask on top of his head, so I did too. "You'll probably do better if you stroke less often with your arms," he suggested. "Let your fins drive you forward, turning your head to the side to breathe. Or you can use your snorkel since we're not racing."

"Okay." I replaced my mask, put the mouthpiece in, and swam a few strokes. My movements were awkward, but I made more progress when I relaxed instead of thrashing. It was invigorating to swim again, though I kept forgetting to breathe only through the tube. I bobbed up in front of him, smiling and panting a little. "Thank you!"

A strange expression crossed his face just before he went under and swam away. My heart hurt a little, but when Fathoms bumped me, I gave him a loving pat. "We'll enter the salt water soon, buddy boy. But no worries. I'll see you again in a few hours." I replaced my mask and resumed swimming.

When I finally reached the rock at the border between the fresh and salt waters, I found everyone but Tor perched on its jagged sides. He waited for me in the salt water, rising and falling with the swelling waves. "Swimming like a human . . . is harder than it looks," I gasped as soon as I took the snorkel out of my mouth.

"This place is amazing!" Nora gazed at the cliffs looming above us.

"My sisters and I named the volcano Mt. Ibu, Mother Mountain, in honor of our mother," I said, "because it spouts smoke whenever she loses her temper." Its slopes were lush and green, a verdant jungle filled with birds and other creatures. When Tor and Jonathan both gave me startled looks, I realized the family joke was too revealing.

Hurriedly I changed the subject. "Next, we will swim around to a secluded lagoon. There's a sandy beach or rocks to rest on, and a beautiful reef, though only half of it lies within island waters. Any castle guests on that shore might see us sunbathing on the rocks, but we can hope they'll mistake us for sirens."

"As if that could happen," Mike scoffed. To make his point, he raised one arm and flexed his biceps. "No siren ever had arms like these."

"I should hope not," I said, then gave Nora a questioning look. She raised a brow and smirked. She had won their race. I wasn't surprised. Mike looked awkward in the water, almost as awkward as I felt. Which made me wonder how many of his boasts had any basis in fact. The man was undeniably beautiful to look at, chiseled muscle in all the right places and near-perfect features for a human, but his social skills were pathetic. Even I, a siren, could tell he was out of place in good society. He tried too hard to impress.

His life story might be interesting to hear. I wondered if he could ever be convinced to tell it. Was he a commoner who had risen to royalty by some romantic means? With a body like that, he must be good at something. He was supposedly heir to the throne, so maybe his people just wanted handsome kings. Stranger things had happened.

"So, Mike, who won your race?" Jonathan asked outright, and I heard a wicked edge to his voice.

The prince frowned, looking broodingly handsome. "If I were at my best, I could have won easily." Then his expression cleared, and he gave Nora a heart-melting smile. "But Nora is an amazing swimmer, and she won today."

"Aww, Mike, thanks!"

Wait. What was this? I had only ever heard Nora laugh at Mike and seen Mike patronize Nora . . . yet just now their facial expressions bordered on soppy.

So, Nora had attracted a handsome prince in less than twenty-four hours, while I could barely coax a complete sentence out of Tor?

Who was the real siren here?

"Ready to head to the lagoon?" My voice held a sharper edge than I'd intended, but no one seemed to notice.

They hopped down into the water, and I led the way, threading the path between volcanic rocks. This would have been much easier in my mermaid form, yet, aside from the matter of Tor, I was enjoying my role in this party of humans. They were all interesting people, and after tomorrow I might never have such an experience again.

The ocean water was warm and beautifully clear. Little pied cormorants dived from the rocks around us—Tor had told me all about these birds years ago, but he wouldn't remember that. Gulls cried overhead, and a turtle paddled alongside us. My friends gasped in delight at its size.

We were nearly to the lagoon when someone screamed in terror. Heart in my throat, I spun about.

14

NELUMBO LOOMED OVER us, his mouth open to reveal those razor-sharp teeth. The beast loved to provoke screams, and I could never blame people for freaking out at the sight of him. How anything so large managed to approach with no warning had always puzzled me. "No danger! He's just showing off."

The screamer, that is, Dr. Benyamina, gave me a disbelieving glare.

I swam over and latched onto one of the spikes on the back of his neck. "I swim like a rock in this form, Nelumbo. It's weird to be in the water without my tail! Thank you for coming, and for keeping sharks away."

My companions relaxed as he rumbled something affectionate.

"You all can sit there to rest." I pointed out a handy basking rock near the lagoon's entrance, and most of the group climbed atop it. The doctor swam toward my lake monster, her eyes wide and wary. "It looks even larger today. What an amazing creature!"

Nelumbo enjoyed admiration. He allowed the doctor to swim around his head and study his spikes, the floppy things that served him as outer ears, and the other dangling growths resembling fungi or fleshy weeds. He could raise these various appendages to make himself look even larger and quite terrifying, but as far as I knew, they had no other purpose.

"Are there many creatures like him in the world's oceans and lakes?" Dr. Benyamina inquired. She was a good swimmer and never seemed out of breath.

"I don't know of any others, but I haven't traveled very much. Anyway, Nelumbo likes his privacy, and I respect that." I gave him a pat and let him loose.

"I would love to know if they mate indiscriminately or choose life partners. How are the young raised? Are they like crocodiles, which carefully tend their young? Or more like snakes or turtles that lay eggs and leave? What does he eat, and how much?"

Something about her forceful questions irked me. "I can't tell you those things. Sorry."

Her brow creased, and she gave me a steady look. When I didn't back down, she turned to Nelumbo and said, "If only you could speak."

He let out a moist, smelly breath and sank beneath the surface. I don't think he cared much for Dr. Benyamina either. This wasn't the first time I'd felt uncomfortable under her cool gaze, as if she were thinking things about me that I didn't care to have thought.

The doctor spun about, using her arms, to face me. "Why did he leave?" she asked.

"Too many questions?" I guessed. "He is easily bored."

"Then I shall direct my questions at you. Will you arrange to introduce me to a mermaid or merman? While I am pleased to have met you, I should greatly prefer to meet one of your kind in proper form."

"I'm sorry, but my sisters don't speak to humans. They would never agree to speak to you."

The doctor frowned, sharp lines marring her brow. "Do you think, perhaps another day, the monster would be willing to let me touch it? I wish I'd brought an ordinary camera like Tor's. I never dreamed we wouldn't be allowed cell phones."

"Ordinary cameras are allowed, but taking photos of the magical creatures is not," I said quickly, "and I wouldn't recommend trying to touch Nelumbo. If he wants someone to touch him, he lets them know."

"This ban on cell phones and other technical devices is unreasonable," she complained sharply. "A place can be magical without insisting on caveman technology."

"I wouldn't know about that."

The doctor sniffed in evident disdain. "Speaking of magic, do you and Mike have a history?" she asked. "He behaves as if he has some claim on you. However, I must say, my niece seems to have captured his full attention."

Something in her tone raised my hackles. "I never saw the prince before he helped pull me out of the lake yesterday. I expect he thinks every woman should be in love with him. Some guys are that deluded."

She gave me a look that seemed to say, "What good are you?" and swam away.

The morning passed quickly. Jonathan and Dr. Benyamina perched on the basking rock and argued, not loud enough for us to discern the cause of their dissension but loud enough to be annoying. Mike and Nora sunbathed on the tiny strip of white-sand beach hidden among large rocks, but Nora quickly overheated in her wetsuit, so they soon joined Tor and me at the reef.

As we floated above the colorful corals, a large octopus wafted up to perch on my outstretched arm, its strange eyes studying me with apparent interest. I couldn't recall meeting it before, but the creature might have observed me from hiding for years, for all I knew. Tor snapped photos with his underwater camera. I wasn't sure any photograph of me would turn out, but he took plenty of the sea creatures as well.

The fish noticed my scent and voice rather than my appearance, and all seemed to accept me as a siren. When a pair of hump-backed dolphins joined our company, the octopus took cover in the coral, so the dolphins amused themselves by tugging at my swim fins. This pleased Mike, who had found it difficult to keep up without fins. But when a dolphin nipped his bare toes, he climbed up on a small rock and sulked. Nora pulled herself up beside him. I could hear them talking at the surface, but I didn't want to eavesdrop.

The dolphins kept sticking their mottled pink-and-gray snouts into anything we did. Tor took many photos of their laughing faces and of me posing between them.

Sunlight glimmered through the clear water, making the corals, anemones, and fish below us glow with brilliant color. It was all so familiar to me, yet it felt strangely alien. Looking into Tor's eyes through his swim mask also felt familiar, yet not.

After a dive, I surfaced for a breath and blew water out of my snorkel. I kept forgetting to use the thing.

Tor surfaced beside me, propped his mask on top of his head, and watched me cough and wipe my nose. It was rather humiliating. As soon as I could breathe properly, he said, "I've been thinking, and I need to talk to you."

"Okay." Something in his tone alarmed me. I glanced around. No one else was near us.

"Do you know how to break this spell that's on me?"

My limbs seemed to freeze up, and I sank. Tor grabbed my shoulders and pulled me back up. "Kamoana, are you all right?"

His voice sounded far away. I could only shake my head. What could I say? We needed to love each other, I knew that much, but how that love was to be measured, I didn't know. A kiss? A proposal of marriage? Did he need to risk his life to save mine? This type of spell had many variations. No matter what I said, he would probably believe this had all been my idea. Honesty was my only hope.

I looked straight into his eyes. "My best guess is True Love's Kiss."

His thick brows rose high. "Seriously?"

He looked distressed, and no wonder. It was rotten of my mother to steal his memories and hold them hostage to involuntary emotions. He still held me up, his big hands gripping my shoulders. Anyone watching us might have mistaken this discussion as romantic . . . if they weren't able to see our faces.

"Sorry to state the obvious," he said, his tone gentler, "but I don't love you."

"I know."

"Is there anything else we can try?"

"Something might happen if we stick together for the rest of your holiday." Like what, I didn't know. He was unlikely to risk his life to rescue me or to propose marriage.

A variety of emotions flitted across his face. "Tell me, who is Mike?" he asked abruptly.

"Prince Mike? He's a prince of some country in North Ordonusia."

"How long have you known him?"

"Since yesterday morning. He helped Beatrice and Eddi pull me out of the lake after I transformed. I'm not very good at swimming in human form, as you've observed." I relaxed in his grasp. He couldn't use his arms to tread water while holding me up, but his flippers were sufficient; he seemed unaware of the extra weight.

Through my wetsuit, I felt his fingers tighten slightly. "He behaves like he knows you. Like he owns you."

My heart rate picked up. Tor sounded as if he didn't like the idea. I tried to smile, but it felt quivery. "I'm under the impression that he makes the same assumption about every woman—we must all be in love with him at first sight. I don't know why he keeps assuming I want to be with him—I've made my disinterest clear. Maybe because I'm a siren?"

Feeling slightly braver, since he was studying me, I studied his face in return, noting the strong jaw behind that short beard. I saw traces of the boy Tor, yet six years had changed him in ways I approved.

How strange it was that I, a siren—raised to view humans as hideous, distorted beasts—had fallen in love with a human boy and still found him attractive as a man! It didn't matter that he lacked scales and webbing. I loved his strong hands and expressive mouth and the thick lashes framing his eyes—they were part of Tor, and I loved Tor. I loved him, therefore he was beautiful to me.

Even as these thoughts crossed my mind, Tor's focus moved from my eyes to my mouth. His eyes widened and his grasp on me loosened. "Uh, we should probably swim again."

"I can talk while swimming, I think," I said, and swam away, paddling with my hands.

He followed alongside me. "You say you remember rescuing us after the shipwreck. How did you happen to be there?"

I explained about the Siren Ball and Kranakoa.

"Did you see the shipwreck happen?"

I chose my words carefully. "I asked Nelumbo to take me to wherever you were. I thought he would take me to see you at the university, where he used to deliver letters from me, but instead, he took me out into the sea and up to the surface in the midst of the storm. I first saw the sinking boat, then the lifeboat. You weren't in it, so I went in search of you."

"The others tell me that Nelumbo rescued them, but you tossed me into the lifeboat and hopped in after me. They couldn't see you until you spoke to them."

I nodded.

He slowed and looked away across the lagoon. "Nora said I. . ." Expressions rippled across his face, but I could not read them. Perhaps if I were better accustomed to reading human expressions, I might not have been surprised when he asked, "What does your tail look like?" His voice sounded gruff, yet I felt oddly encouraged.

"It looks blue in the light."

He nodded. "What will happen if we can't break the enchantment?" He swam alongside me again, using a sort of sidestroke so he could see my face, but mostly he saw it in brief glances. Did he feel shy? Embarrassed? How could I know?

"You will go on as you are, with no memory of me—except possibly for whatever time we spend together now."

His face went still, and he was silent for several strokes. When he did speak, his voice was so quiet I almost missed the question. "And you? What will happen to you?"

"I assume I will return to being a siren."

Again he was quiet for a time. We swam parallel to the shore, looping around the lagoon.

"Why wouldn't you want your old life back?" Tor asked.

I couldn't speak, but I looked directly at him. My expression must have supplied the answer.

"Because of me," he said quietly. "And I can't even remember you. I mean, sometimes I have flashes of what might be memory. When you spoke of the turul . . . Did we see it together?"

"We escaped from it together."

He nodded, deep in thought. "We were good friends?"

"Yes." The best, I thought.

"We studied fish and birds together, didn't we? I guessed that when you took us to see the ducks."

"You once asked me about goldeneyes, so I have always watched for them to nest here. You taught me to like birds, and I challenged you to study fish."

"No kidding?" For a moment he looked happy. "Crazy, but this information is filling in blanks I've wondered about for years. I've always wanted a friend who shared my obsessions." He gave me a bright look, but then his face darkened again. "But someone took that friendship away from us. Some evil wizard or witch."

15

I HELD MY TONGUE. My mother wasn't evil, and no one would dare call her a witch to her face, but her method of keeping control of her youngest daughter could use some refinement.

"We were just kids then," he continued, "so why didn't I come back to Faraway Castle every year? I came only two summers, the second time when I was seventeen. I can't imagine staying away if you were here."

Something in his tone encouraged me.

"Wait," he continued before I could speak. "How long ago were my memories stolen? If I remembered you at the shipwreck and acted as crazy as everyone says . . ." He shook his head. "I don't get it. How old was I when we first met?"

"Sixteen. I was fifteen."

"And we wrote letters to each other over the winter, and Nelumbo delivered them. How did he get them to me?"

"I don't know. You two worked that part out. You sent me scientific journals and used textbooks as well as letters, always wrapped in waterproof bags."

He shook his head in wonder. "Did you and I fight that next summer?"

"No."

"We did see each other though."

I nodded.

"Your expression tells me it didn't go well. If we didn't fight . . ." He looked away, then his gaze jerked back to my face. "We were caught. I'm right! I can tell by your expression. And my memory of you was stolen!" He frowned. "Which would explain why I acted so irrational at the shipwreck. My memories must have come back that night—I had a big lump on my head and a concussion. Might a blow to the head break a memory suppression?"

I was convinced that the sound of my voice had broken the spell, but without waiting for an answer he continued, "So, once I recovered, I came here, excited out of my mind to see you again. All those stories my friends told me make sense now."

He was doing an amazing job of figuring all this out. My heart caught on the words "excited out of my mind to see you." I must have been just as eager and thrilled to see him.

"And we were caught together again, and my memory was stolen again." He gave me a considering look. "And you were changed into human form." Thoughts flashed through his eyes.

Then he gave me a direct look. "No matter the motivation for this spell, I know when I'm being manipulated. The person who stole my memory disapproves of our friendship?"

I nodded.

"Was the memory thief the same person who turned you into a human woman?"

"I have no memory of being transformed, but I have every reason to believe so."

Frowning, he nodded. "I need to think about this for a while." He flashed me a rueful look that changed into a genuine smile. "My mind boggles at the realization that I had a teenage crush on a siren. How many guys have a mermaid girlfriend?" His face sobered. "I mean, it wasn't just a friendship thing on your part?"

I could only look at him with my heart in my eyes.

His expression softened. "Oh, wow," he breathed, then swallowed hard. "Okay. Yeah. Even more to think about. You do realize that I'm an egghead, a guy who can hardly talk to women, let alone ask them out. I live with fish and birds and books and computers, and when I'm not buried in a lab or writing papers, I spend most of my time underwater or in jungles or on mountainsides. And here I am babbling nonsense at . . . the most beautiful woman I've ever seen. Who is a siren under an enchantment." He heaved a deep breath. "It's a lot to take in."

"Hey, you two, the rest of us are starving." Jonathan shouted across the lagoon. "If you don't come, we're heading back to the boat without you."

Fathoms met us just past the rock, eager and wriggling. It struck me then that if I did succeed in winning Tor's love in the next few days—an unlikely prospect—I would have to leave Fathoms behind, maybe only dropping in for visits at the lake now and then.

I wrapped my arm around the fish's thick body and gave him an affectionate squeeze, even though he kept getting in my way while I tried to swim. I was swimming so much slower than usual, he probably thought I was injured or something.

While we ate our sack lunches in the boat, heading back to the castle, Tor was quiet. As his silence extended, my chest began to feel hollow, and every breath seemed to ache. Two dramatic rescues and a brief teen romance. Most of it long in the past. Should I give up my life—the only life I'd ever known—for that? What would I become? Where would I live? If Tor wanted to marry me, what would his family say? I was a princess in my world, but in the human world my title would count for nothing.

I glanced at Tor seated across from me again in the bow. He knew I wanted him to love me, to kiss me. He knew that someone had wanted me to give up on him enough to enchant us both and force the issue to an end. He held my future in his hands, and he didn't care much for the responsibility. I couldn't say I would have felt different had I been in his position.

The fact that he might leave with his colleagues in two days filled me with panic.

I felt his gaze on my face more than once before we reached the dock, but the boat was no place to continue our conversation, and afterward I hurried off to find my human friends.

Instead of taking a nap that afternoon, I trotted around the castle grounds with Beatrice and the indefatigable Princess Edurne Zuri, who seemed to know every person under twenty by name, including staff members and children. To be honest, it was a relief to be away from the university crowd for a few hours, though I kept a sly eye out for Tor.

Which was foolish, I told myself as we girls headed to the castle to dress for dinner. He was unlikely to be anywhere away from the lake and his colleagues. Did the man have any interests outside of scientific studies and diving? I had seen no evidence, if he did.

As I prepared for the evening, including an after-dinner concert in the gardens, I couldn't escape the tormenting fact that two of my designated three days were gone. "Before the sun sets on the third day . . ." Or maybe, if I was lucky, the deadline would be midnight. Both times seemed impossibly close.

But what more could I do? I had already foisted my company on Tor several times. Should I invite him to the Summer Ball tomorrow night? I didn't know how to dance on human feet, and I had a feeling he was no dancer either, but maybe he would be willing to hang out with me for those few hours.

I pulled open my lingerie drawer and glimpsed a flash of gold. Tor's ring. I held it up before my eyes, and memories flooded through me—memories of his fist opening beneath mine, his eyes bright with unspoken love and sadness. I fastened the chain around my neck and let the ring lie just below the hollow of my throat. It felt right, as if it belonged there. What would Tor say when he saw it? He might well demand its return, and I could not refuse. I shook my head and unclasped the chain. I should offer to return it in private, not wear it openly.

When Eddi, Beatrice, and I arrived in the dining hall, the scholars were nowhere in sight, so we took seats at an empty table. We all wore pretty dresses—mine was sleeveless with a flowy skirt in shades of green and blue. It felt cool and soothing at the end of such a busy day. This time we all brought wraps for evening.

135

I was destined for disappointment. Tor did not come to dinner. The rest of the university crowd joined us, but I recall none of the conversation. Only Beatrice's urging convinced me to attend the concert. I do remember that the gardens were lovely and so saturated with magic that even my dulled perception felt dazed, but the music left no impression on my memory. I could think only of the looming deadline.

Mike and Nora sat together and wandered off on a garden path after the concert ended. Jonathan and Dr. Benyamina invited me to join them for a stroll down to the lakeside, but I refused. The last thing I wanted was another grilling from the scientist or unwelcome stares and compliments from her assistant. I felt relieved when they left together.

By the light of radiant sunflowers, Beatrice and Eddi chatted with friends. With one hand in a pocket hidden in the fullness of my skirts, I fiddled with the gold ring and chain. I could either seek Tor out tonight or return it to him in the morning. Maybe I should just head back to my room and try to get some dreamless sleep. As I turned toward the castle, I saw the outline of a tall man standing a short distance away in an arch of shrubs, the glow of magical flowers reflecting in his eyes. "Tor?"

He stepped forward, and I could see him more clearly. "I spent the afternoon thinking," he said. "A lot. I know I haven't been very good company, but would you . . . Could we spend a little time together now, tonight, and see what happens?"

Hope is a painful thing. It seemed to squeeze my heart in a vise. "I . . . I would like that."

His shoulders dropped a little as if in relief, and I realized he was as tense as I felt.

Slowly I held out my hand—a risk, but it paid off. He stepped forward and took my hand in his. "I believe that is the entrance to a maze," he said, pointing to the place he'd been standing. "It's lighted with flowers like little flames in all different colors. Want to explore it?"

"Sure! I've never been in a maze. What do we do?"

"We're supposed to find the center. There will be lots of dead ends and wrong turns."

"Let's solve this thing!" I said and squeezed his hand.

He grinned, white teeth visible in his shadowed face, and my heart turned over. I'd begun to wonder if the man ever smiled!

Above us, stars lighted the sky, with a bright patch above the mountains where the moon would soon appear. We entered the maze together, side by side. Tor's hand was large and warm. In my memories his hands were always wet and cold, since as kids we'd spent most of our time together in the water. "Left or right?" he asked when we reached a T.

"Right." We set off. "I have no idea, but I figured a confident decision couldn't hurt."

"Except when it leads to a dead end," he said when our path abruptly ended.

As we wandered and laughed, sometimes running, sometimes meandering, the awkwardness between us dwindled. Then I noticed a distinct pattern in the tiny lights in the maze's walls. "Let's try following the green lights," I suggested.

And it worked. We took a few turns and arrived in an open square surrounding a fountain. Water spouted from the mouth of a sea monster much like Nelumbo but subtly feminine, her tail coiled around a large rock. Fish rose to greet us as we approached, their mouths sucking at the surface, their tails waving. "Good evening," I greeted them.

"Do they understand you?" Tor asked.

"Maybe." I smiled. "I think they hope to be fed."

"Is this a food dispenser?" he asked.

It stood to his right, and I felt certain it hadn't been there a moment before. Tor twisted the knob until fish food dropped into my palm, then he filled his own hand.

We sat on a curved bench beside the pond and tossed food into those sucking mouths. The sky was now ablaze with stars and moon, dark only where the mountains blocked our view. While we sat there, large white flowers twined over the back of our bench and gently glowed, allowing me to see Tor's face. "They look like moons," I commented.

"Probably moonflowers," he said. "Though I doubt most moonflowers glow like these do or smell half as nice."

"I must thank the castle gardener," I commented, gazing up at the brilliant stars. "I never thought anything on land could be as pretty as a coral reef or a school of fish dancing in sunlight, but this pool and garden make a memory worth keeping."

"If you're allowed to keep it," he said, and my joy vanished. He didn't remember dancing with those fish. He might never remember.

"I'm so sorry," I almost whispered. "It isn't fair."

He laid his hand over mine on the bench between us and squeezed gently. "I don't blame you anymore, Kammy."

16

MY HEART GAVE a jolt. "You called me Kammy."

"Do you mind?" Tor sounded hesitant. "I think of you that way."

For a long moment I couldn't speak. "You always called me Kammy back then."

Another silence. "It suits you." He kept his hand over mine. "I no longer suspect you of enthralling me, Kammy. I see your frustration, and I know it's genuine. Someone is manipulating you as well as me."

I looked down into the pool where the fish now drifted in replete contentment. My other hand slipped into my pocket, and I grasped the chain and ring in my fist. "Tor, hold out your hand, please."

He did so. I set my fist on it, then uncurled my fingers. The ring and chain dropped from my grasp. "What's this?" He released his hold on my other hand as he lifted the ring to the glow of a moonflower bobbing over our shoulders. I clasped my hands together in my lap, waiting.

After a brief study, he glanced sharply at me. "Did I give this to you? I thought I had lost it in the lake."

"You did lose it in the lake. I found it that first summer and returned it to you. It was your grandmother's, you told me." I stared at the fish or my fingers or the stars. Anywhere but at him. Already my throat was so tight, I could scarcely speak.

"Why do you have it now?"

"You gave it back to me the next summer, just before your memories were stolen."

He sat there with the chain dangling from his fingers, staring at me. "Did you wear it? Do you still?"

"Around my neck, yes. But only when I am alone. I have never dared let my family see it."

He turned to stare at the fishpond and said, "Kammy, when I first saw you yesterday, I felt cursed, hunted. I was convinced you must be shallow, selfish, and cruel, because sirens never love humans; they only play with them as cats play with mice before the kill."

"It's true," I said. "Sirens treat human men like prey." I clenched my hands and drew a long, shaky breath.

Tor continued: "But then I saw that Miss Beatrice de Callen had befriended you, and I respect her judgment. She seems convinced your story is true. And instead of collecting a string of mindless male followers, you went out of your way to avoid them—you even encouraged that Mike guy to like Nora. And . . . I would expect a mermaid to know something about fish. But birds? You're a true birdwatcher, I can tell. Last of all . . ."

Tor folded the ring and chain into his hand, crossed his arms over his chest, and leaned back on the bench. "I didn't tell you earlier today, but I can't help seeing the connection between my few remaining memories of visits here those two summers when I was a kid and the things you say we did together. How would you know any of those details if you hadn't been there? Omar tells me I called Nelumbo by name last week. Everyone else here calls him the lake serpent or monster. And Fathoms . . . I remember him too. And the turul, and the pine tree where it nearly killed me. The only thing missing . . ." He huffed a sigh and turned to me ". . . is the most important of all. I'm sorry I don't remember being in love with you."

"That is hardly your fault."

"I'm not apologizing. I mean I'm wretched. Miserable. That kind of sorry." He cleared his throat. "You've got to understand: I don't do relationships. Either the girl isn't interested, or when I try to start something, it feels wrong, so I back off." He looked directly at me. "Have I been waiting for you?"

"I hope so," I said barely above a whisper.

His teeth flashed in a brief smile, but then fear and reserve returned. "Why? Why me? I'm often a jerk and always a know-it-all. Sure, I've got a title, but so does just about every other man here. Every man in the world would want you."

This last statement distressed me. Did he still see only my appearance?

He groaned, bent his head, and rubbed his beard. "I'm making a complete mess of this. What I want to say—what you must have noticed tonight—is that I'm willing . . . no, *more* than willing to spend time with you, to give this a try. The idea scares the daylights out of me, and when I'm not with you I think I must have lost my mind, but . . . there it is."

"Thank you," I whispered. His offer was more than I had expected, yet would it be enough?

"I've got reservations for another week here after my colleagues leave, and my time is yours."

Time? I opened my mouth, but words would not come. Something stopped them. Something that was not me.

I should have known. The three-day deadline must remain secret.

I rose quickly, turned, and offered him my hands. "It's late, and we have tomorrow," I said with as much cheer as I could muster.

He let me pull him to his feet, and his hands gripped mine. His eyes were wide, and I heard his breath come short. For a moment I dared to hope he might kiss me, but I wasn't surprised when he didn't. I admired his patience and restraint. I wouldn't want him to be anyone else.

No kiss, but he kept hold of my hand and linked our fingers. Just as he had once before, long ago in the lake.

"Goodbye," I called to the fish.

"We might be back here in a minute if we get totally turned around," Tor added.

But we walked directly out of the maze into an open, grassy lawn dotted with great, spreading trees. Everything looked different than how I remembered, but things often do look different in the dark. "How large is this garden?" I asked.

"I don't know, but I don't think it goes on as far as it looks."

"I always wondered what lay beyond the castle," I mused aloud. "It is very beautiful, this view."

"It's different every time I see it," he admitted. "Always beautiful, but the inconsistency can be disconcerting. It wasn't like this—this magical, I mean—when I came as a kid."

"There are still other people out here. Let's just walk," I said. "I have a feeling we'll be at the castle doors before we know it."

"Like, it's programmed to return us to the castle at a certain hour?"

"I bet it does. I think this garden likes its privacy."

After a brief pause, he cleared his throat. "What do you say to taking a walk to the pine tree where it all began?" he asked. "In the morning, I mean."

My heart skipped a beat for joy. "I say let's do it! Do you want to go to the Summer Ball too?"

He paused, gave a self-conscious laugh, and said, "Yeah, okay. I'm no dancer, but . . . yeah."

Hands linked, we planned out the next day as we strolled across the velvet sward, listening to the calls of night birds, never once hearing the hum of a mosquito. It was too perfect for words. Too perfect to last.

"What are your future plans, Tor? What will you do when you leave Faraway Castle?"

"I'll resume work on my thesis. It's been approved, and I'm about halfway through writing the paper now. I've presented it in a few places and received some excellent feedback." He looked up at the stars, then glanced toward me. "The human world understands so little about the magic creatures living around us, and too many react entirely with fear rather than attempting to learn how we might peacefully share the planet. I recognize now that my knowing you undoubtedly inspired the passion I have for conserving the magical and mythical beasts of this earth. I wish . . ."

His voice trailed off, but then he resumed his train of thought. "No matter what happens with this spell, I hope to keep in touch with you in future, to discuss important issues. I mean, if you could tell me what merpeople think, how we might connect the governing bodies of both worlds, to help them work together for the good of all . . ."

I let him ramble on, all too aware that my mother would never allow me to communicate with a human after I returned to mermaid form. She might even remove me from his memory one last time. In no way would I be part of Tor's life.

". . . Dr. Benyamina keeps talking about studying merfolk from life, and I keep telling her we can't study sentient beings the way we study whales or sea turtles. Not without causing magical incidents. I don't think she understood that merfolk are equal or superior to humans until meeting you."

"She keeps trying to convince me to take her to meet my sisters," I told him. "Nothing I say convinces her that she would be most unwelcome. Only by direct invitation from a sovereign can a human visit a mer palace or community. To attempt such a visit uninvited would be suicidal, and I lack the authority to issue an invitation."

Tor shook his head. "She and I clash often. Our methodologies in studying wildlife are widely divergent, and when sentient beings enter the picture, the gap grows wider and deeper than an oceanic trench."

He stopped walking, and I looked up to see Faraway Castle's main entry ahead, which was quite impossible. "You were right. I don't know how, but here we are," he said quietly. "I suppose it is getting late, and you have undoubtedly heard more than enough of the political side of scientific studies."

"Not at all. I find your work fascinating, and I'm grateful and pleased to know that you are a champion in the human world for the rights of magical creatures." I let go of his hand

and shifted my grasp to his arm. He immediately bent his elbow and straightened his shoulders.

"May I escort you to your room?" he asked, sounding hesitant.

"Yes, thank you." He might claim his social skills were rusty, but I appreciated his efforts to please me.

The portico and lobby were dotted with people, mostly couples saying their goodnights or laughing groups of friends. More laughter, music, and talk came from one of the public rooms where a party seemed ongoing. The elevator was unavailable, so we took the stairs. Our footsteps echoed up the stairwell, and my legs were cramping up by the time we reached my floor. "Is your room on this floor?" I asked as he opened the door into the hall.

"I'm one floor up." He briefly met my gaze, and I knew this was all new to him—escorting a woman to her door. "I'm sharing my suite with Jonathan. Last night he came in hours after I'd been asleep and crashed around in the sitting room. I won't feel at all guilty if I wake him up tonight."

I found my key, and he took it, unlocked my door, opened it, turned on the lights, and gave the room a quick scan. "Just to be safe. Faraway Castle is secure, but a young woman can't be too careful in this world." His voice was very deep. He handed me the key and turned to go.

"Tor," I said, then faltered. He turned and stood there, so tall and straight, his cheeks flushed, his eyes bright. "Thank you for tonight," I said. "I enjoyed myself very much."

His Adam's apple bobbed as he tried to swallow. "So did I. Kammy . . ." He paused and swallowed hard again. "Don't give up. Please. I mean, I've only known you since yesterday—I mean, according to my memory—but I . . . you . . ." He gave a little laugh and shook his head. "You're amazing." His face was scarlet, and he could hardly look at me.

"I've always found you amazing, Tor," I said. "I look forward to tomorrow."

His eyes flashed up to meet mine. "I do too. Good night."

As soon as the door closed behind him, I burst into tears. He was so sweet—just larger, stronger, and better educated than the Tor I used to know and love. Given time, he would come to love me, I felt certain. But by tomorrow night? I could only hope and pray.

I slipped into a pair of silk pajamas decorated with tiny unicorns, wondering who picked them out. I brushed my hair, then my teeth, turned out the light, and climbed into my big, soft bed. Would this be the last time I slept in a dry bed with blankets?

Sleep was slow in coming. I tried to focus on the promised walk in the morning, but hopes and worries kept creeping in. One day was not enough, and—especially since he didn't know about the deadline—I couldn't blame Tor for taking things slow. He was being wise.

What would Mother do if I outright defied her? She could be tyrannical but never deliberately cruel; she would never force me to marry Prince Pike. After a little time passed, I could possibly find Tor again—with help from Nelumbo—during his future underwater explorations. I might be able to shake loose a few memories Mother had overlooked.

A nice thought, but of course it was hopeless. I sighed and rolled over.

And soon fell into another dream . . .

17

VOICES FLOATED OVER me, and a cool breeze ruffled hair across my face. I raked the tickling strands back with my fingers and squinted up at a clear blue sky with mountaintops at its edges. I lay on my back beneath the warm sun, my tail curled to one side.

"I tried that recipe for kelp puffs last night, but they didn't turn out like yours. Did you leave out an ingredient or something?" my sister Coral grumbled.

"Why would I do that?" Moselle asked, unruffled. "I don't play petty little games."

"Oh, and I do?"

"Stop trying to pick a fight, Coral," Talulah butted in. "It's too nice a day for a brawl."

"I'll gladly explain how to make them again." Moselle sounded the most like Mother of any of us, authoritative and confident, but she always meant well.

While my three sisters bickered, my thoughts rolled back over the past few days and weeks. A month had passed since the

Siren Ball, a month I'd spent fending off Prince Pike's proposals, all the while hoping Tor would soon return to Faraway Castle. Last week, Mother had dragged me, against my will and despite my clearly stated protests, to Onterrica, the vast chain-lake kingdom of King Burbot in North Ordonusia, for almost a week's stay in the royal palace. Only yesterday, I had refused yet another proposal from Prince Pike the Puerile Paragon.

How could Mother honestly claim to be surprised? Pike wasn't villainous or hideous or anything like that. But not only was he unbelievably self-centered, he also scorned my scientific interests and refused even to consider allowing his wife to pursue further studies. Why would any siren desire a career when she could while away her days admiring and praising the magnificence that was Pike?

Thirty minutes in his company was provoking. Five days was purgatory.

The entire time we were there, I fretted and worried that Tor would arrive at the castle during my absence, search for me in vain, and believe I had forgotten him. Last night, almost as soon as I got home, I swam to the covered landing at the castle portico and called to Sten, the dwarf working at the front desk. He informed me that Tor had arrived and spent the entire day either on the lake or walking around it. I panicked. Had he been calling for me?

To my relief, Mother was due to attend yet another council meeting and would be away for a few days. Perfect! I slept fitfully, rose at dawn, and planned to haunt my favorite rock all day.

Only to discover that Mother had asked my sisters to keep me company—code for spy on and nag me—during her absence. So here I was, trapped on Siren Rock at the southeast tip of the island with Moselle, Talulah, and Coral, hoping for a glimpse of Tor but afraid even to glance toward the castle while three pairs of suspicious eyes watched me.

"Last of all, you whip the seaweed pulp until it's light and fluffy, then fold it gently into the salmon eggs," Moselle explained in her patient tone.

"I did all that, but mine got thick and gummy, and Turbot didn't like it," Coral complained. "Whenever I try your recipes, they never turn out right. I think I'll stick with my urchin-roe bites."

"Wrasse likes to take me out to exotic places instead of making me prepare our food," Talulah said in her most superior tone.

"La-de-da." Coral flipped her hair over one shoulder. "You think you're so fine. But when Kamoana marries Prince Pike, she will eat in the palace dining hall with servants waiting on her every day."

"*When*?" Talulah echoed. "You mean *if*. At the rate our baby sister is going, she'll be living here at the island with Mother until they're both old and gray."

They were my half-sisters, but despite having different fathers, we loved each other—and bickered—like full sisters. I couldn't imagine having grown up without them around to make sure I scrubbed algae from my teeth and combed crustaceans from my hair.

Moselle, the eldest, had black hair tipped with copper, and Talulah's hair was white. From their father, Black Drum, those two had inherited perfect ebony skin and scales that gleamed green and violet in the light. Pale-skinned Coral, her hair and tail a bright orange with black tips, was the only child of her father, Garibaldi. Of the four of us, I looked the most like Mother, with ordinary blue-black hair and light-brown skin, but she always said my tail reminded her of my father, Bluefin.

Moselle poked my tail with a sharp fingernail. "Wake up, Kamoana. Are you listening at all?"

"I hear, and I would far rather live out my days at Palau Kalah than marry Prince Pike."

Without opening my eyes, I pictured their expressions as they heaved angry sighs.

"But why?" Coral whined. "You could marry the most sought-after bachelor of the century, yet you refuse him again and again. What is wrong with you?"

"He's a decent guy, I suppose, but I don't love him," I said. "I told him so yesterday. He may ask me a hundred times, and I will give him the same answer. I don't care how handsome he is; he bores me to death. Nelumbo is a better conversationalist, and Pike has no respect for my interests and values."

"But he is devoted to you," Talulah said.

"I beg to differ; he is devoted to Prince Pike. I wouldn't be surprised to see him puff out his gills and threaten to attack his own reflection in a water window." I pushed myself upright and stretched my arms and shoulders, using the opportunity to glance around toward the castle.

There were humans on the beach and several boats on the water—sailboats, canoes, and a power boat towing a skier. The skier it towed took a jump off the ramp in fine style. I squinted at him—was that the prince Nelumbo disliked so much? I hadn't seen him on the lake in years. But I couldn't tell; the sun's glare was too bright and the distance too far. Tor could be out there right now, and I wouldn't know.

"I say Mother should have erased Kamoana's memory after she rescued that human boy," Talulah said, combing through her silvery hair with her long fingernails. "She has never been right since. Always studying birds and drawing pictures and keeping records of fish hatchings. As if anyone really cares! Do fish hatch more fry because she keeps records?"

Coral giggled. "She needs to settle down with Pike and raise some small fry of her own. Then she won't be so curious about the private lives of trout and carp."

Moselle snorted in amusement, shaking her thundercloud of hair. "Mother has to work with magical human men on the council, but most of us can avoid looking at them too closely. All that skin! And hair! So effeminate. Males should never have hair."

Talulah laughed, tossing her own hair over her slim shoulders. "Human beasts are fun to catch and release, but I never want to get too close to the ridiculous-looking creatures. Who could admire a man with no scales or fins?"

"I could," I said. "Appearance isn't everything, you know. Tor was my friend. We talked about our common interests."

Coral snorted, but Talulah turned to look at me, her brow wrinkled in concern. "You don't still think of him, do you? I mean, a siren couldn't possibly care for a human in a romantic way. They're so . . . ugly!"

Just then Moselle, who had the sharpest eyes among us, sat upright on her tail. "Oh girls," she sang out. "We have a potential victim!"

We turned to follow her pointing finger. The ski boat was much closer now; it was Moselle's target. "Are you sure that's a man driving?" Coral asked.

Even as she asked, the skier did a cartwheel in the air, his skis flying off in opposite directions, and hit the water with a smack. I gasped in concern, but a moment later his head popped above the surface, and the boat circled back to pick him up.

"I'm sure," said Moselle. Despite her talk of human males being too much like females, she never mistook one for the other. "Target the driver."

My sisters burst into song, Moselle taking the lead in their dissonant yet lovely chorus. Magic flowed across the water, circled the boat, and wrapped itself around that foolish driver's head. The boat turned away from the skier and now roared directly toward the island. I saw only the one person on board. So, two men had taken out a resort boat with no women aboard and no spotter, and then water skied near the island. Several major rules broken at once. The man deserved what he had coming, but it seemed a shame to smash up a brand-new ski boat.

Sunlight shone like gold on the driver's short hair and beard. He wore sunglasses and a tank shirt and . . . My mouth dropped open. It was Tor!

I snapped my mouth shut and glanced at my sisters. They all three balanced on their tails, heads back with hair flowing in the breeze, their arms outspread as they sang their discordant spells with evident delight.

Coral's voice rose above the others in a destructive enchantment, and a whirlpool formed in the boat's path. The boat was doomed, but Tor would simply go for a swim until a lifeguard picked him up. Or . . . What if I snatched him and swam through the water door to some hidden lake across the world?

It hurt my heart to see Tor ensorcelled by my sisters. Only a man in love with a woman could resist a siren's spell. Tor must not care as deeply for me as I cared for him.

Coral's harmony shattered. "My whirlpool!" she wailed as Tor spun the wheel and the boat skirted the magical whirlpool. "He can see it!"

That shouldn't be possible! The ache vanished, and my heart thundered in my chest. Tor was not enthralled; he was coming for me!

Moselle then flung her arms and her voice to the sky, and a great wave followed the boat. But the boat accelerated with a roar, and the wave crested and broke behind it. Its swell carried the boat up onto the beach, then receded.

And there sat the boat, listing slightly to one side, high and dry on the white sands. Its engine turned off, and Tor hopped out.

My sisters fell silent, their mouths agape.

Tor climbed the sandy bank. From its crest he studied Mt. Ibu, then turned toward Siren Rock. He lifted his sunglasses, stared our way for a moment, and replaced them on his nose.

"He sees us," Moselle moaned.

"Of course he does—we called him!" Coral wailed. "But he resisted our spells—all three of us!"

"He must be a *sahir*," Talulah snapped. "I don't know about you, but I'm getting out of here." And she dived into the waves pounding our rock.

"I don't sense magic on him," Moselle said, "but my wave couldn't catch him."

"And he avoided my whirlpool. What will Mother say?" Coral clutched her head with both hands.

Moselle turned to glare at me. "Since you were no help at all, you go tell that human to get off our island if he values his life. You've talked to humans before."

"Yes! Get rid of him, but please don't tell Mother we failed to enthrall a man," Coral cried. "And especially don't let her know he walked on Palau Kalah. Such an intrusion has never happened before. Ever!" She made a sudden flip with her tail and disappeared into the water.

Moselle reached over and gripped my arm. "We're counting on you, Kamoana. Don't mess this up! Get that man off the island before anyone sees him—human or fay!" She jumped. I saw her iridescent tail give one flick underwater, and she was gone.

I finally dared to look for Tor, but he was nowhere in sight. Had he not recognized me? I couldn't follow him on land, and I didn't dare call to him. I slipped into the water and headed toward the beach where the boat lay stranded. How would he get it back to the castle? I wondered if I could conjure up a wave to lift it off the beach. But I had never attempted anything like that before. I would probably end up smashing the boat and Tor with it.

Aside from the boat, the beach was empty. Tor must have walked across the point toward the lagoon. I swam around the southeast tip of the island, up the west shore, and crossed the reef into the lagoon. Tor was there, standing in the water—I could see his feet and lower legs. His deep voice seemed to float on the waves: "Kammy? Kammy, are you here?"

18

I POPPED MY HEAD above the surface. "I'm here, Tor." I had to push hair back off my face.

He pulled off his sunglasses, and I saw his eyes, wide and wondering. "Kammy!" I couldn't hear his voice, but I read my name on his lips.

A wide smile transformed his face, and he took another step forward, soaking the hem of his knee-length shorts. I swam closer until my tail touched the sandy bottom with each stroke. "Why did you come to the island?" I asked.

His smile scrunched into a grimace. "Desperation? I couldn't find you yesterday. Fathoms found me, but you didn't answer my calls. Today, Omar wanted to go skiing, but our driver didn't show up. No staff members were around, so we took the boat out. After he fell, I heard sirens calling me and decided to answer whether they liked it or not, on the chance you might be with them."

"What happened to your friend? I didn't see."

"Nelumbo knocked him down. I saw a lifeguard coming to pick him up. He'll be fine. I knew Nelumbo wouldn't hurt him. Kammy, I've got to talk fast, because I know they'll come after me. I plan to sneak out tonight; I brought along my own wetsuit and fins. Meet me at our old place?" He nodded toward the shore where we'd met so often as teens at a large rock with a cleft in its side like a seat wide enough for two.

"But now they'll think you're siren-spelled," I said.

He shook his head, frowning. "You're right. I should have worn my wetsuit today. We could have swum off together now, and they wouldn't have found us for days." His mouth twisted into a half-smile. "Kammy, we've got to find a way to be together. We have years to catch up on."

This felt so awkward. I wanted to hug him, but shyness held me at a distance. "I know. I have research to show you, and I've been hoping just maybe you could teach me some of what you've been learning at university, like you promised that summer."

"I remember." Even in the bright glare of summer sun, the glow in his eyes was nearly blinding. "I remember everything now. It's been like . . . like getting out of prison, or maybe out of an insane asylum. All these years, half of me has been missing and I didn't know what was wrong." He took a few more steps forward until he was up to his waist in water and reached his hands toward me. "I could swim off with you now. I mean, I'm not dressed for serious lake swimming, but we could maybe snatch an hour or two before the lifeguards find me."

The buzz of a lake scooter interrupted his last words, and the little craft whipped around the point leading into the lagoon. I instantly recognized its driver as the Gamekeeper's assistant, the girl with the magical voice. Before she could speak to me, I dove underwater and zipped through the lagoon out into open lake water.

I didn't hear the lifeguard's voice, but I heard Tor. "Kammy," he cried, "don't forget!" The hint of desperation in his deep voice made me want to cry. I moved into the shadow of a large rock and watched as Tor walked stiffly up the beach in the direction of the beached boat. His unnatural gait told me that the lifeguard had used her magic on him. I disliked the idea. If it was wrong for sirens to control people, why was it okay for her to do it?

I swam around to the east side of the island in time to follow the boat; another lifeguard drove it while Tor sat in the back, unmoving. At the castle dock, two male staff members waited to escort him to the castle. He cast a glance over his shoulder toward the island before disappearing into the trees lining the path. The lifeguard's compulsion must be wearing off.

The humans couldn't steal his memories, I knew, but they might use other means to keep him from returning to me. What could I do? He could enter my world, but I could never follow him into his.

Recalling my promise, I waited for him at our rock all night long. He never showed up. In the morning I swam to the landing outside the castle's main entrance and dared to scoot up on shore until I could see into the lobby, which was quiet and dimly lighted. Only Sten the dwarf sat behind the desk, reading and yawning. I waved, but he didn't look up.

All that day, I waited and watched for any sign of Tor. Had they sent him away from the resort just for setting foot on the island? How could I know? I asked Nelumbo and Fathoms to be on the lookout for him. No news.

I spent that night on Siren Rock, staring up at the stars. Sometime after midnight, a thick fog crept over me and surrounded the island—my mother's work, for sure. I swam out to the center of the lake and looked back. The entire island was shrouded in magical fog. Everywhere else was clear.

Had one of my sisters told Mother about the man walking on our island? No, more likely the resort director, Madame Genevieve, informed her. The lifeguards who escorted Tor back to the castle—there had been more than one—were required to report everything to do with us sirens, and Madame relayed to Mother anything connected with the island.

It was early morning when I popped awake on the rock, disoriented in the fog, and stiff and aching from sleeping out of water. Had someone called me? I sat up, feeling dehydrated, and scooted to the edge to dip my tail into the water.

"Kammy?" The voice sounded muffled in the fog.

"Tor?" In an instant I was underwater and headed for his voice.

But I heard shouting, men's voices, and then a series of crashes. Frightened and cautious, I swam a weaving path between rocks, listening for more shouts. But all was silent now.

Then I saw someone floating in the water, someone wearing a life vest. "Hello? Tor?" I asked before considering that the hair was too dark and long.

The man spun around and let out a yelp of fright. It was the water skier, Tor's friend.

"You are Omar. Tor has told me about you." I tried to sound friendly and harmless.

His eyes were round with fear, but he nodded. I noticed that pieces of what looked like a yellow kayak bobbed in the water around him, and a paddle floated near a rock. I wondered . . . but I didn't ask.

"Don't worry, you'll be fine. Someone will come and pick you up. I need to find Tor." I paused. "You must forget that you saw me." Yes, I confess: I infused my voice with magic to make him forget. But from now on he would see magical creatures; that couldn't be helped. He turned and swam away through the mist.

"Kammy?" It was Tor's voice somewhere nearby, sounding strained and sharp. "Kammy, are you here?"

I followed his voice through the mist and found him hauling a kayak up on the shore. As I watched, he pulled off his life jacket and tossed it into the kayak. He wore a short wetsuit, and water shoes instead of swim fins. Standing on the beach, he cupped his hands around his mouth and called again, "Kammy!"

"I'm here, Tor."

He turned, spotted me instantly, and charged out into the water. I swam to meet him in the shallows, and this time, with no hesitation, he scooped me up into a hug. Someone less sturdy than a siren might have been crushed by that embrace. But when I pushed on his chest, he loosened his hold. I grasped hold of his bare arms, and his big hands supported my elbows. "Kammy. Kam, they gave me a drug, an anti-siren-spell injection."

I believed it. His eyes were dilated, his voice sounded thick, and he had a wild, reckless look.

He shook his head as if trying to clear it. "I told them I wasn't siren enthralled, but they wouldn't listen." His speech pattern was uneven, the words coming in bursts. "This morning I knew I'd forgotten something important, something at this island, so I took the kayak, and as soon as I got here, I remembered your name. Kammy!"

He seemed to be in pain—tendons strained visibly in his neck, and his arm muscles were like rock against my hands.

"What happened with Omar?" I asked.

"He tried to stop me, so I smashed his kayak. I won't let anyone stop me. I . . . I won't!" He pulled me to him again, and I hid my face in the curve where his shoulder met his neck. I felt the effort it cost him to think, to fight against the magical drug. "Please, please take me somewhere," he begged, "somewhere across the world where they can't find me and can't take you away. My life without you was empty." He swallowed hard, then grimaced and said, "Kamoana, please!"

"Oh Tor!" Tears flowed from my eyes, tears salty like seawater but glowing with my emotions. They dripped on his neck as he held me to him, and I soon felt him relax. His arms held me with tenderness instead of desperation. When he lifted his head and I looked into his eyes, they were no longer wild.

"Your tears soothed the pain," he said. "Is it magic?"

I reached up to touch his dear face. His whiskers brushed my palm. He was a man now, no longer a boy. His voice was deeper, his body much stronger. Yet the boy I loved was there in his eyes. "Maybe it is."

He lifted one hand to my face, still holding me with his other arm. His fingers trembled as he smoothed hair from my cheek and forehead. I saw his eyes focus on my mouth and knew he wanted to kiss me.

But just then, the throb of a boat's engine drifted through the fog. "Lord Magnussen, are you there?" It was Madame's stern voice.

Tor's jaw hardened. In one swift motion, he picked me up so that my tail hung over his arm. It was awkward and uncomfortable, but he held me easily enough with the water supporting some of my weight.

"Kamoana, are you hiding that human?" I heard the director call. "You had better show yourself now. It will be the worse for you if you delay. You know very well that you cannot keep a human. It is never allowed."

I looked up at Tor, and he met my gaze with a defiant look. "This human wants to be yours," he said quietly. We gazed hungrily at each other, studying features, memorizing details, while the boat idled past, invisible in the mist. But it was not enough. I knew my time was short.

"Tor, my mother will come and steal your memory again," I whispered, laying my hand alongside his face. "Please fight the spell!"

He turned his face toward my hand. "Kammy, I—"

A blinding flash made Tor stagger back, and I clutched him around the neck just as a new voice spoke, reverberating amid the rocks, echoing from the cliffs and the waves: "Enough of this."

Dazed, Tor turned to face the shore, trailing my tail in the water. Then he gave a yelp of surprise. "What is that?"

Queen Pukai stood on the shore, and at her side stood a broad-shouldered figure with gills flared and mouth gaping. Prince Pike.

"Kamoana!" he cried, his round amber eyes nearly starting from his head.

"Hello, Pike. Good morning, Mother," I said, nodding regally from my position in Tor's arms. "You recall Torbjørn, Lord Magnussen of Hyllestad, I'm sure."

Mother's face was serene, but Mt. Ibu rumbled and fire spurted into the sky, turning the mist red and gold.

"Jaya," Queen Pukai called past us to the director in the boat, "head to my cave. We'll soon put an end to this nonsense." With one sharp gesture she lifted the fog, and bright sunlight nearly blinded us. Her dark eyes focused on Tor and me as she said, "Now."

Water and wind began to whirl around us, whipped into spray and foam. Clinging to Tor with all my strength, I felt the waterspout lift us, together, into the air.

19

THE RUSHING WIND and water carried us across the island to Mt. Ibu, straight through a wide waterfall that fell in a translucent sheet from a sheer cliff, and into the entrance of Mother's council chamber. The waterspout pulled us apart and dropped Tor, none too gently, into a metal chair made by humans, then swept across the chamber to drop me into one of the pools dotting the black stone floor. Its mission accomplished, the waterspout ceased swirling and poured neatly into another pool.

Each of these pools was a doorway from the network of cave chambers beneath the island. Without bothering to surface, I hurried through familiar underwater passages and popped up in the pool closest to Tor's chair. There I perched on the ledge surrounding the small pool and rested my elbows on its side while taking stock of the situation.

Aside from the pools for merfolk, the great stone chamber held benches, tables, and more chairs to accommodate the land-dwelling enchanters Mother frequently hosted. High above, its black ceiling glistened with reflections like a faceted mirror of darkness. To my left, beyond Tor, the floor sloped up to the wide doorway we had entered, which shimmered like a water door, a trick of the eye caused by the waterfall. Its proximity should have made conversation nearly impossible, but a perpetual spell hushed the water's roar to a gentle purr.

Water puddled beneath Tor's chair. His wetsuit had short sleeves and reached only to his knees. Water trickled down his hairy legs and arms as he sat forward, elbows on his knees. More water dripped from his beard. As I watched, he gave his head a shake and sent spray flying.

Then he sat upright and looked around, taking in the waterfall, the ceiling, the pools, and me. Without a word, he rose, picked up his chair, brought it to my pool, and sat down within my reach. He held out his hand, and I slipped mine into it. We sat there holding hands and awaited our fate together.

On a platform across the chamber, Madame Genevieve, Pike, and my mother seemed unaware of our actions, involved as they were in deciding my future.

Correct procedure was the conflict, I gathered, listening with half an ear. Pike argued in favor of bringing in the resort's Gamekeeper to ensure lawful process. Madame Genevieve argued against such a move. "This is a merfolk matter and none of his business!"

"The Gamekeeper would handle this efficiently and fairly," Pike began, but Mother cut him off.

"Are you saying I would not?"

Pike paused only an instant. "No ma'am. Could you not hear me? I am known for the clarity and resonance of my voice. I said—"

Mother closed her eyes and drew a deep breath. "I heard what you said."

Leaning slightly toward me, Tor spoke from the side of his mouth: "I've been in this cave before."

I nodded with sorrowful gaze. Six years ago, almost exactly. I pressed the back of his hand to my face, and the corners of his mouth turned up. "This will turn out right," he said.

"The proper person to handle this minor problem is Queen Pukai," the director was saying, her tone even colder than usual. "The offender is, after all, her daughter. She knows what must be done."

"But the human is a guest at Faraway Castle," Prince Pike pointed out. "Do you have authority to decide the penalty for this kind of infraction? Does Queen Pukai? My father would—"

"Enough." Mother's word effectively cut off discussion. "I shall handle this, Your Highness, and you will say nothing to the Gamekeeper without my permission. Understood?"

Pike's stiff, scaly face could not scowl, but his tone expressed dissatisfaction. "Yes, Your Majesty."

Mother glanced toward the pool she'd dropped me into. Finding it empty, she scanned the room until she located us, still holding hands. I pushed myself up to perch on the edge of the pool and leaned my cheek against Tor's arm. He gently squeezed my hand.

Sirens are beautiful, as everyone knows. But Queen Pukai is possibly the most beautiful of all. In her human form she isn't tall . . . unless she decides height would be advantageous. On this day she wore four-inch heels and a slinky green dress that glistened like her tail. Her black hair was loose, flowing past her hips as she walked toward us with the sinuous grace of an eel.

Releasing my hand, Tor rose and bowed respectfully. Not too low, not too shallow. Despite her heels, he towered over her.

Mother never reveals anger. Never. But on that morning, twin lines appeared between her perfect brows. Ignoring me, she focused on Tor. "I thought I dealt with you permanently six years ago."

He met her gaze in unflinching silence.

She turned her cool, contained fury upon me. "How did you break through my Forget spell?"

"I'm not sure I did," I answered honestly. "Tor took a blow to the head, I rescued him from drowning, and he remembered me."

"When was this?"

"Last month, in the Begaian Sea."

Queen Pukai blinked twice. "The Siren Song Ball . . ."

"So that's where you went!" Prince Pike approached us, his webbed feet slapping on the stone floor. "You left me at the dance to go rescue a human? Why?"

I looked him in the eye. "I left you at the dance to search for Tor, but I didn't know about the shipwreck. My timing was fortuitous. I happened upon Tor and his colleagues just after their boat sank in that storm."

Pike tilted his head and gave Tor a fish-eyed stare. "Huh," he grunted. "He's not half the man I am, human or merman."

Tor was half a head taller, but Prince Pike's ego was blind to such trivialities.

"Merman. Is that what you are?" Tor took in Pike's olive-green complexion, creamy belly, and scaly, fishlike head. Pike's webbed arms and hands could be viewed as human-like in shape, and from the waist down he was shaped like a human man other than webbed brown feet emerging from slim-fitting breeches. He was lean and powerful and had sharp teeth like his namesake fish.

166

Queen Pukai was lost in thought. "That spell never fails. Did you speak to him again after I expressly forbade it?"

"The first time he heard my voice was when I called his name while trying to find him in the storm," I answered firmly. "That's when his memories returned."

"What difference does any of this make, Pukai?" Madame Genevieve snapped. "Stop talking and just get rid of him."

"You shouldn't question matters you don't understand, Jayachandra," my mother said without looking at her. Strange. I had heard her call the director "Jaya" before—I had thought it a nickname—but never this long name.

"I understand this matter better than most," the director snapped, her voice more animated than usual. "And don't ever call me that again! Why are you wasting time? Erase the human's memory of Kamoana and send him back to the castle. Marry your immature daughter to the prince and have done with this ridiculous drama. Are you the *sahira* queen or not?"

Mother slowly turned to regard her, lips pursed. "This is my daughter, my problem."

As the two women faced each other, I noticed a similarity in their stances, their profiles. But . . . that was impossible.

As Madame Genevieve held the siren queen's gaze, her eyes widened.

A slow smile spread across Mother's face. "So that's your fear!" She glanced at me, then back. "Perhaps I should offer my daughter the same sporting chance you were given. It seems only fair."

Although pale, Madame Genevieve spoke firmly. "Nonsense. I learned a terrible lesson about the peril of entertaining unhealthy passions, and I still suffer the repercussions. I cannot undo my own mistakes, but I can pass on the wisdom I gained. Do not play games with your daughter's future as you did with mine, Pukai. Kamoana should remain in her own world."

Mother went very still, and I felt the room's temperature drop several degrees. "'Play games.' Is that how you recall the matter now? How interesting. I remember a girl who scoffed at the very arguments you now offer and demanded my help."

She then turned to look Tor up and down. "The man is a baron, I have heard, and heir to extensive properties, but otherwise unexceptional."

Her cool dismissal of Tor infuriated me. "He is exceptionally intelligent, hard-working, and honorable, Mother."

Her brows twitched upward. "Is he indeed?"

Prince Pike broke into the discussion. "Your Majesty, this human has dared to set foot on your island and pay court to your daughter, my betrothed. Since you insist on administering justice yourself, what is your decision?"

The queen's lips curled upward at the corners. "The temptation is nearly irresistible. Why should my daughter not be offered as much chance as my sister had to win her heart's desire?"

Sister?

"That 'chance,' as you call it, ruined my life."

Mother lowered her chin and gave the director a level stare. "If your life is ruined, which statement is dubious, your own pride is at fault. You took an outside chance and failed. There is no shame in that. But afterward you refused to return home, admit failure, and move on with life. Nearly thirty years have passed, Jaya, and still you cling to false pride. I will gladly return your mermaid form even now if you so choose. Our people would welcome you back with open arms."

The director . . . my aunt? . . . went very still, and her green eyes gleamed with fury.

The questions flooding my brain almost distracted me from the present crisis. The director had loved a human? Who? When?

"It is unfair," she stated bluntly. "Kamoana has advantages I lacked."

Mother turned her focus back to Tor, pressing the tip of one red-polished fingernail beneath her lower lip. Her equally red lips curled in an unpleasant smile, and her dark eyes glinted with humor. "To humor you, Jaya, I agree to place a handicap on these two."

Years ago, Tor had stood before her, trembling yet bold. Now he didn't so much as flinch under her contemplative gaze.

"This deliberation has gone on long enough," Pike said, his voice resounding through the cave. "Send the human back where he belongs and give me Kamoana as my wife. She will be happier than she can imagine."

"That is the wisest plan possible, and you know it, Pukai," the director seconded.

My mother turned to face the merprince. "Why do you wish to marry my daughter, Your Highness?"

I believe Pike would have blinked in surprise had he possessed eyelids. "What?" he blurted. "Why do I . . . ? Because she has always been destined to marry me. There can be no better match for your daughter or for me. You and my father agreed on this when we were children."

I thought I saw Mother grow slightly taller as I watched. "Yet I do not force my daughters to marry; the choice is theirs. Kamoana remains unconvinced that you are her future husband."

Pike's mouth gaped in shock. "But my father the King—"

"Your father is not here, and I do not believe he would contradict my statement."

No one contradicts Queen Pukai. Pike was speechless—a rare occurrence.

"But you are wrong! If Kamoana does not remain in her own world, she will never feel at home anywhere," the director declared.

Okay, so *almost* no one contradicts Queen Pukai.

"I appreciate your concern, Jayachandra, but this is my daughter's story, not yours." Mother again regarded Tor. "How old are you, human?" she asked.

"Twenty-three."

"What do you do with your life?"

"I am working on my doctorate in the magical-natural sciences. My thesis is on the history and future of magical birds and sea creatures. This includes rocs, turuls, and phoenixes as well as krakens, kelpies, and selkies." Tor's confident tone filled me with pride.

"Where do you study?"

"I worked and studied last year at the University of Neoncheo, on the east coast of South Ordonusia. Currently I am composing my doctoral thesis through the University of Barbacha, a major center for magical oceanic studies, where I took my undergraduate and one of my master's degrees."

"What exactly do you hope to accomplish after you achieve this doctorate?" Mother spoke with apparent scorn, yet I could tell she was impressed. So was I. When it came to his field of expertise, Tor spoke with confidence and eloquence.

"I hope to make the human world more aware of the treasures these magical beings truly are. Some of them are dangerous, yes, but those creatures are being kept under control by responsible enchanters. I hope to help the non-magical creatures as well by educating humans about better ways to dispose of waste products such as paper and plastic."

Her scornful tone vanished. "Commendable. I rather expect you will make a mark in this world and effect positive change. Where does my daughter fit into these plans?"

"Your daughter and I enjoy studying the same subjects, and she was my original inspiration to add fish and other ocean creatures to my interests. She once shared your late husband Bluefin's records and journals with me—a tremendous privilege—and during my undergraduate studies I became acquainted with the renowned scientist Dr. Marofit, who claimed Bluefin as a friend and colleague and mourned his tragic though heroic death."

I saw Mother's eyes widen slightly, but she said nothing.

"Even after my memories of Kamoana were gone and the doctor retired," Tor continued, "my oceanic studies far outstripped the study of birds: I obtained my first master's degree in ichthyology, the second in ornithology. If you will allow your daughter to remain in contact with me, I would like to involve her in my work to improve human/magical relations. Her contributions would be invaluable."

He paused, swallowed hard, and added, "I love your daughter and would be honored to marry her if we could figure out a way to make it work."

"Interesting," Mother said.

I saw my aunt and Pike stiffen in outrage, but they kept silent as my mother turned to me and said, "Kamoana, I am contemplating an action I have not attempted in many years." She glanced at Tor. "This human's devotion to you is remarkable. However, I cannot evaluate at this time how much of this declared love is mere passion triggered by your proximity, magic, and beauty. You two knew each other as teens for a matter of days and exchanged a few letters, and now you believe the attachment you then shared to be lasting love. But in the past six years you have both grown from children to adults, and you have both changed. What will you think of each other as adults and strangers?"

"Tor and I have cared for each other through six years apart, Mother," I said with an edge to my voice. "How much more lasting can love be?"

"Have you considered a lifetime of marriage to a man you cannot sleep beside? A man who will die if he is trapped in your world? What of possible children? The complications of such a match are incalculable. I intend to test you. Both of you," Mother replied smoothly, and I heard the director suck in a breath.

"What?" Pike cried, his fisheyes nearly popping from his head. "What about me?"

"Oh, you may be part of it, if you so choose." Mother sounded pleased with herself. "How delightful it would be if, after all this turmoil, Kamoana were to choose you!"

"Your Highness?" said a little voice.

No one but me seemed to hear it, and the others kept talking. Tor looked back at me, his expression puzzled yet faintly hopeful.

"Your Highness, wake up!"

". . . at the end of the third day," Mother was saying.

But the scene in the cave grew fuzzy, the voices indistinct. I heard Tor say, "But three days is unrealistically fast. I don't make decisions quickly."

"More's the pity for you then" was Mother's response.

"Your Highness!"

My eyes popped open. Two small brown faces stared down at me from inches away. Brownies. "We're sorry, but Sten asked us to wake you."

"Sten?" The dwarf who worked at the front desk. "Is something wrong?"

20

I STRUGGLED UPRIGHT, BLINKING in the bright sunrise pouring through my windows. "What's going on?" Flashes of that scene in the council cave kept appearing before my eyes. I could almost feel the stone floor under my tail and Tor's hand in mine.

The brownies now gazed at me from the foot of my bed. Brownies always look mournful, but these two seemed particularly worried. "We don't know what is wrong. Sten can't leave the desk untended, so he sent Kai to talk to you. He's waiting in the hall."

Kai. Princess Eddi's dwarf friend. My brain was starting to function again. Slowly.

Mother's cynical yet eager expression. Pike's amber eyes and gaping mouth. The director's fury and . . . pain. My mother's sister? I couldn't deal with that thought and shook it from my mind.

Tor. What had she done with him?

A picture of his closed, angry expression during that first boat ride with the university gang appeared in my head. Not once but twice now, my mother had invaded Tor's head and suppressed his memories of me. The effrontery, the invasion of privacy, the *cruelty* of this suddenly infuriated me anew. That my mother would do this to the man I loved—it was beyond bearing.

Less than a day remained of this test . . . no, curse. Might as well name it accurately. If Tor didn't love me by the end of today, everything would end—our friendship, my dream of studying science and making a difference in the world at his side, pretty much everything that mattered most. I flung my feet to the floor and stood up.

"We'll tell Kai that you're coming," one small messenger said.

"Thank you . . . um, Sira and Jig, right?"

Their faces lit up. "You remember us, Your Highness?" Jig cried.

"I told you she would," Sira, the older brownie, said calmly. "We'd best be on about our work. Many more rooms to clean yet this morning!"

They both vanished.

I dressed, brushed out my tangled hair, then hurried to open my door. Kai waited in the hall, his expression stern. I ignored the glamour and looked him in the eye. "Is something wrong, Kai?"

He straightened quickly and bowed. "We hope not, Your Highness, but Sten is concerned. Late last night, before he went off shift, three guests walked out of the castle, three of your acquaintances. People had been coming and going all evening, what with the garden concert and all, so he thought little of it. But when Sten returned to the desk this morning, the night gate guard told him that a car is missing from the guest parking area, though he didn't see anyone drive away. The castle's night clerk never saw those three guests return to the castle. The brownies who clean the guest suites confirm that in two suites one bed is empty, and the prince's suite is entirely empty."

"A prince? Who all is missing?"

Kai produced a slip of paper and read the names: "Dr. Saliha Benyamina, Mr. Jonathan Howell, and Prince Michael of Dorintosh." He offered the paper to me. "Here are their suite numbers."

I took it, blinking and trying to think. Why would those three have walked out together, let alone left the resort? Foreboding tied a knot in my belly. I didn't trust Dr. Benyamina or Jonathan, though I couldn't imagine their purpose in kidnapping a prince. It didn't fit, somehow. "Has anyone questioned the other members of their party?"

"Lord Magnussen and Miss Rachid are still sleeping," Kai said. "We all thought you were the best person to alert. Sten hasn't yet informed the director."

I nodded. "I'll go try to roust those two. Thank you, Kai. I'll get word to Sten."

Moments later I knocked on a guestroom door. Beatrice answered at my knock. "Good morning, Kamoana. You're early today." She was dressed already, her hair smoothed back into a thick bun. "We saw you with Tor last night and are hoping for a fun update." Then she paused, her brow knitted. "Is something wrong?"

I quickly filled her in on the disappearances. "I need to talk to Nora and Tor, but I hoped you might come along. Is Eddi awake?"

"She hasn't come out of her room yet. I'll let her know where we're going, all right?"

Minutes later, with Beatrice at my side, I knocked at the door of Nora's suite. No answer. I knocked harder. Still no response.

"What should we do?" I asked.

"You still have your siren magic, don't you?" Beatrice asked.

"Yes, but it's limited."

"How about your voice? Can you focus your siren voice on one person?"

"I never thought of trying," I admitted. "I'm not sure if I can speak to Nora when I can't see her, but I'll try."

Beatrice described the layout of the suites. "Try the smaller room. It would be right about there." And she pointed at the wall.

I carefully focused my voice in that direction. "Nora, wake up."

Beatrice gave me a curious look. "You didn't make a sound."

"I did, but it all went to Nora. I hope."

We tried knocking again, and this time I heard thumps and bumps inside the suite. Then someone fumbled with the doorknob, and it slowly turned. Nora's face appeared, her eyes heavy-lidded and bleary. "What?" she groaned.

We both stared. "What happened to you?" Beatrice asked.

"I feel . . . drugged." She rubbed both hands over her face. Nora without her smile looked innocent and vulnerable.

"Where is your aunt?" I asked.

"Probably in her room. Come on in." She staggered backward and nearly fell over.

Beatrice hurried to peer into the larger bedroom. "It's empty. The bed hasn't been slept in."

Nora leaned against a table and rubbed her face. "I feel awful. My tongue feels thick, and my head is buzzing."

I met Beatrice's sober gaze. "We need to check on Tor," I said, my heart starting to race.

"Drink a lot of water to flush out the drug," Beatrice advised Nora before we left.

We hurried upstairs to the suite Tor shared with Jonathan and repeated the knocking and my focused call. "Tor, it's Kammy. Please come to the door. Something is terribly wrong," I said.

This time the response was quick. Tor flung open the door and stood swaying on his feet. "Kammy. What's . . ." Bleary-eyed, he stared at me. "You're all right?" He glanced at Beatrice, then looked back at me.

He wore baggy plaid pajama pants and a threadbare tank shirt. "Tor, do you know where Jonathan, Dr. Benyamina, and Prince Mike went last night?"

His eyes closed and opened slowly, painfully. "No. Why?"

"They are missing."

He slowly turned and walked from the entryway into the suite's small sitting room, where he stopped at an open doorway and leaned his shoulder against the frame. "Jonathan's not . . . in his room." He rubbed one large hand over his face.

I followed him into the suite without invitation and checked the bedroom. The curtains were shut, yet I could easily see that the bed had not been disturbed and the open closet was empty.

"Tor, did Jonathan have any chance to slip you a sleeping drug last night?"

His heavy-lidded eyes met my gaze, and I saw comprehension dawn. "He made hot chocolate right after I came in. It tasted bitter."

Beatrice followed us into the suite, leaving the hall door ajar. "Nora was drugged too. Kamoana, the brownies said Mike's suite is entirely empty, right?"

"Yes. We might want to take a look and maybe find some hint where they went."

Despite the situation, I couldn't help appreciating how sinewy and strong Tor was . . . even as he rubbed his eyes with the heels of his hands and blinked hard. He was no charmer like Jonathan or gorgeous hunk like Mike, but I enjoyed looking at him, beard and all. Love worked its own magic, it seemed.

Beatrice went to the galley kitchen and drew a glass of water, which Tor drank in a few gulps. "Thanks."

"Knock, knock?" Nora peered through the open door. She looked slightly more awake now and was fully dressed. Seeing us gathered in the sitting room, she walked in. "Jonathan is missing too?" she asked Tor, who nodded, then winced and went very still.

"Feel as if a horse kicked you in the head and dragged you through a desert?" She gave him a commiserating look. "What's going on? Who drugged us, and why?"

Tor's face darkened, and he suddenly seemed more alert. "When did any of you last see Mike or Dr. Benyamina?"

"Mike left me at my room around eleven, I think," Nora said. "My aunt gave me some hot chocolate, and we sat talking . . . I don't recall going to bed."

"At times like this, I wish telephones worked here." Tor's voice still sounded thick. "Or any kind of electronic communication device."

Beatrice nodded. "The director must be informed. This is an incident for the Council of Magic to handle, and Madame Genevieve can contact leaders in the magical world."

Including my mother.

"What do you mean, 'an incident'?" Nora asked. "What happened?"

"Apparently Dr. Benyamina, Jonathan, and Prince Mike left the castle last night," I said, "and they haven't returned."

"And a car is missing from the parking area," Beatrice added.

"They took Mike?" Nora's voice was nearly a whisper.

"Give me a minute to dress." Tor took a step, swayed on his feet, and amended the request. "Make that five minutes."

We waited in the sitting room, which was clean though cluttered with Tor's scientific equipment and papers. "When we came here, Jonathan brought all his things in a backpack," Nora said. "So did my aunt." She dropped into a chair and clutched her head with both hands. "I can't believe they would do this," she moaned. "How can they possibly imagine they'll get away with it?"

"Get away with what?" I asked. "Where do you think they went?"

"They kidnapped him," Nora said. "Whatever they told him, the big idiot fell for it." Her voice held unmistakable fondness as well as frustration and fear. Two large tears rolled down her cheeks.

I looked to Beatrice, but she said nothing, her eyes wide. I turned back to Nora. "Why would they kidnap Mike? It makes no sense! I agree with you that they can't possibly expect to get away with kidnapping a prince. What will his people say? This could mean war! Certainly an international incident of the first degree."

Nora gave me a funny look, but just then Tor emerged from his room, clean, neatly dressed, and wearing black-rimmed glasses. "Lead on, ladies," he said with a courtly little gesture.

My heart gave a little flip. "Your glasses!" They brought back the Torbjørn of my past. Studious, serious, and shy.

"My eyes are too sore for contact lenses," he said, but smiled at my pleasure and took my hand in his.

"I'm sorry to desert you, but I must stay with Princess Edurne," Beatrice told us. "She's my responsibility, and I wouldn't be much help in this rescue anyway." Her face revealed genuine regret. "I hope you can find and rescue Prince Mike."

I was sorry to leave her, but it was true she could have contributed little real help. "Thank you for being there for me," I said as she parted from us in the hall.

"My pleasure." She waved, glanced at my hand linked with Tor's, and gave me a thumbs-up. I wasn't quite sure what it meant, but I returned the gesture.

21

MINUTES LATER, TOR, Nora, and I crowded around the desk in Madame Genevieve's office. With difficulty I kept from staring at the director's face as questions flooded my thoughts. My aunt? Seriously? She had never behaved like a loving relative, for certain. Why did she hate me so much? For that matter, why did she seem to despise every pretty female guest at the castle? Had she really gone through the same three-day test? On purpose? Details of my dream danced in the back of my mind, but this was no time to ponder their meaning.

I watched Madame's face while Nora explained about the missing people, and I saw dismay and guilt settle over her usually rigid features.

"Not Prince Pike!" she whispered.

"What?" I said. "What about Prince Pi—Oh!"

Those last moments in the cave . . .

"Pike? Is that his real name?" Nora asked. "He never would tell me."

I felt as if a whale's flukes had whacked me on the head. "You . . . You knew he was a merman?"

While wiping a tear from her eye, she gave me an impatient glance. "I figured that out straight off."

"And he knew that you knew?" If Nora could tell without use of magic, how had I been so blind?

She nodded. "He told me your mother turned him human so he would have equal chance with Tor to win your heart."

I felt my face go hot again. Hearing the plot spoken before so many people in plain words made it feel so much worse. What was Tor thinking? I didn't dare look at him.

But then I recognized the sadness in Nora's eyes. "How could you tell he wasn't human?" I asked. "I had no idea."

She gave a choking little laugh. "It didn't take a sleuth to figure that out. He hated wearing shoes, he never knew how to dress properly, he got a kick out of flaunting his beauty and seeing all the human women—he even called them that once—drool all over themselves. He constantly talked about not being at his best and told me I should see him when he's himself. He ate mostly seafood and complained about any spices, and he has no clue about anything going on in the human world."

With the director's cold eyes upon me, I felt stupid. "Oh." Of course. The same boundless ego, the same boasting, the same expectation that all women would desire only him. If I'd paid even minimal attention, I should have guessed, magic or no. "Guess I'm not the sharpest sawfish in the sea."

Nora gave a wistful little laugh. "You are just as clueless about the human world as he is, but at least you don't exhibit your beauty, and you never tried to fool anyone."

Seeing the sorrow in her smile, I said with all sincerity, "I'm sorry about dragging you into this . . . this mess."

"You didn't drag me in; I came here eagerly, and I wouldn't have missed it for anything! You never did a thing to make me jealous. Mike . . . Pike did that all by himself. He was confident you would fall for him and kept talking about how you two were made for each other. I knew from the start that you cared only for his lordship Torbjørn here, but Mi—Pike wouldn't listen."

"Back on topic," Tor said, sounding impatient with our chatter, "please tell us why you think your aunt has kidnapped him? We all know of her interest in magical oceanic creatures, but kidnapping a merman is extreme. Not to mention illegal in every possible sense. What could be her goal?"

Nora grimaced. "Ever since the shipwreck, Aunt Saliha has been particularly obsessed with finding out about the merworld. She's the one who pushed you to get us an invitation to come here. I thought she simply wanted to meet Kamoana and thank her. But she acted so strange . . . Just yesterday I heard her ask Pike if his magic is really in his bones."

"In his bones? What a strange question! Do humans actually believe that?" I asked.

"Apparently my aunt read somewhere that merfolk magic is located in the bones," Nora said.

"That's ridiculous!" I cried. "Magic is in every cell of our bodies, as it is with every magical creature and human."

Tor's jaw muscles looked taut as he turned to Madame Genevieve. "We must rescue Prince Pike quickly. This crime could have global consequences."

The director nodded, her expression dark. "I'll notify the Council of Magic."

"You need to notify Queen Pukai right now," I said. "This situation is her doing. She needs to know first. Besides, we need her help."

Tor added, "We've got to intercept them before they get Prince Pike to Dr. Benyamina's research lab. I believe they intend to harvest his bone marrow—they're trying to steal his magic."

Nora inhaled sharply and lost her healthy color. "Mike!" she cried softly.

"They won't kill him. At least, not intentionally," Tor told her.

For once Madame Genevieve didn't argue or interfere. She turned around and opened a water window with one wave of her hand. "Pukai," she said, "Emergency situation."

The window, a sheet of water suspended in the air like a mirror, resembled the water doors we merfolk travel through, but it was only a viewing screen. Since Mother was one of the enchanters in charge of Faraway Castle's protection, it made sense that she would provide a water window to Madame Genevieve for quick communication. It shimmered, and Mother's face appeared, looking impatient. "What is it now, Jaya?" she snapped. "I am quite busy."

"Prince Pike has been abducted by humans intending to steal his magic," the director said. "We must notify his father immediately."

There was a moment of shocked silence before Mother exploded. "We must do nothing of the kind! Do you want to start a worldwide magic war? If you say one word to that idiot King Burbot, so help me, I'll—"

Then Queen Pukai noticed me and Tor and Nora. Her eyes went wide, and her mouth snapped shut.

"We need your help, Mother," I said without preface. "Two human scientists kidnapped Prince Pike, and we suspect they will take him to a research laboratory and attempt to steal his magic by removing his bone marrow using surgical means."

"Dr. Benyamina's lab is near the University of Barbacha on the Begaian Sea," Tor added.

Mother's expression shifted from anger to bewilderment to horror. "By removing— That is barbaric! Who would do such a thing?"

"My aunt," Nora said bravely. "She is a minor *hembez*, but she has always wanted to be a great sorceress. If she could steal magic from other creatures, she thinks she might become powerful and rich." She sighed. "I've always tried to believe the best of Aunt Saliha—she is my only living relative. But I'm done. Anyone who would harm Mike . . . Pike . . . is lower than an oceanic-trench worm."

I watched my mother's face while Nora was speaking. Her eyes had the fixed yet twitchy look that meant she was thinking at light speed. "They will travel south by the least traceable means," she said.

"They took Dr. Benyamina's car," Tor said.

"They must be headed to Santa Cyrilla," Mother said. "In an automobile, about an eight-hour drive. From there, they will take a ship to the Mutipan continent." She looked us over. "You three would rescue him?" Her tone held a trace of doubt.

"We will," I said.

"You'll need help." Her tone was firm.

"We'll accept help," Tor answered quickly.

She gave a quick nod. "Then here is what you must do," she said in her most queenly tone.

Within the hour, Tor, Nora, and I stood on a rocky shoreline of Faraway Lake in a cove out of sight from the castle or docks. The morning sun was warm on our heads and sparkled on the tranquil water. I felt overheated and clumsy. We all wore our wetsuits over regular clothes.

Tor carried a large waterproof bag and had bulky waterproof pockets strapped to his legs. "You look like a commando," Nora commented. "Where did you get all that stuff?"

He gave her a grim smile. "Nowadays when you dive off the coast of Neconcheo or any disputed territory, you almost have to be a commando. Hope we don't need weapons, but I'm not going into this unprepared. Are you ready?"

We both nodded. I wondered if Nora was as frightened as I felt. She didn't look it. But she did look determined and worried. About Mike? But she knew the prince as an impossibly perfect human, not as the merman he truly was. She was likely to find him as revolting in his merman form as I had first found him in human form. But then, if she really cared about him, the way I cared for Tor, maybe she could adjust to Mike as Pike and even find him attractive.

Would it hurt Pike's feelings if Nora thought him hideous in his true form? Or was his mind capable of grasping that anyone could view him as less than perfect in any form? More to the point—did he care at all what anyone else thought?

Nelumbo's head rose from the water in the center of the cove, mottled green and brown like algae. "You know the plan?"

I asked him. Not that I needed to. Mother was nothing if not efficient. He gave me a toothy grimace then turned his back on us and waited.

"Here we go," I said, and we waded down the rocky beach, swam to the lake monster, and arranged ourselves on his neck . . . back? Hard to tell with a serpent. "Ready?" I asked my companions. They both nodded, clinging with hands and legs to the serpent's long, curved spikes. Tor had wedged the bag between a few spikes then crouched over it. "Be prepared in case he submerges right away," I said. "I don't know what he'll decide to do." This time I had to be ready to take a quick breath and hold it, just like the humans.

Nelumbo swam on the surface, his long body undulating like that of any water serpent. We encountered no boats—many guests were probably still at breakfast—but a few people on the walking trails stopped to stare in disbelief. Nora waved, and one guest gave a weak wave back.

"So much for secrecy. That story will be all over the resort by noon," I said. "Three people riding the lake monster."

Palau Kalah soon loomed before us. I wondered briefly if my sisters would dare to return anytime soon for more siren-calling. Mother seemed to be unaware of their blunder last week. It really hadn't been my sisters' fault that Tor ignored their siren calls.

The significance of this suddenly struck me. Only a man who was already in love with a woman could resist the call of a siren. Magic couldn't be fooled, so Tor really must be in love with me somewhere under this curse. But without his kiss, I would return to human form and that love would never be fulfilled. I glanced at him riding along beside me, his gaze scanning the slopes of Mt. Ibu. He looked determined and serious, yet I thought he also looked happy. This was an adventure, and he obviously enjoyed a challenge. Did it make a difference to him that I was involved?

When Nelumbo stopped, I could see the glow of the water door far below the surface. "We're right above it," I informed my friends. "Nelumbo will dive almost straight down when I give the word. Take a big breath and hold on tight."

They both were experienced divers, and I had frequently traveled through water doors, yet this was a new experience for all three of us. I placed my swim mask and firmed my grip on those slippery spines. "Ready." Deep breath. "Set." Another breath. "Go!" I sucked in air and held it.

Nelumbo dove smoothly, and I had no trouble clinging to his spines. With my feet tucked beneath two long spikes and each hand gripping one, I felt relatively secure. The water went from green to dark very quickly, with the water door gleaming before us like quicksilver. Then we were through. I didn't feel a great difference in temperature, but my skin sensed the change in salinity. My lungs were aching already, and I knew it would be a long way to the surface. I felt the pressure on my ears change, and my vision went dark. Just when I thought I would surely pass out for lack of oxygen, Nelumbo burst through the surface, and I sucked in a deep breath of sea air.

Once my vision cleared, I discovered that Tor held me by one wrist. I looked into worried eyes behind his mask. "You looked . . . I thought we might lose you down there," he said, his voice rough.

"I'm all right now. I'm not used to holding my breath," I admitted.

"I don't suppose you've had reason to hold it before." He slowly released my arm but held my gaze. "Are you sure you're all right?"

Actually, I was struggling to breathe for a new reason, which was foolish, because he would have shown as much concern for anyone. Wouldn't he?

Nora seemed unaffected by the dive. "Whoa, look at the ships and boats! And oh, wow! Check out that castle!"

Tor blinked and looked away, and I felt trembly in every limb. But there was no time for weakness. We were in the Begaian Sea at the seaport of Santa Cyrilla.

22

CLUTCHING OUR GIANT serpent's spikes as he bobbed in the warm, sparkling sea, we stared in awe at beautiful cliffs, islands—one bearing an ancient castle—a huge port lined with ships, and a shining city rising behind it. All shimmered in the heat, though it was still hours from midday.

"Mother said to purchase tickets, but where?" I asked. "This port is vast! And we can't ride our sea monster in there without attracting attention." I already sensed something watching us. Friendly or unfriendly eyes, I couldn't tell.

"Yeah, we should probably swim," Tor agreed. But we hadn't brought swim fins, and he had that heavy pack to carry.

"We need to get ashore in an out-of-the-way place," Nora said, "like that one." She pointed to a rocky bit of shore below what looked like a path or road.

"Good plan." Tor pointed toward three or four large ships painted in different designs. "And those ships look like ferries. We can walk on the road from that point to the docks." He patted our serpent's scaly neck. "Nelumbo, please take us to that rocky point to the left."

While our serpent slithered onward, I still stared at the row of ugly ships. "The ships look like fairies?" I didn't even know how to ask what he meant.

"F-E-R-R-I-E-S," Nora explained, laughing. "Ferries. Ships that ferry people back and forth between two places. Not magical creatures."

Tor lost his tense expression long enough to grin. "Sorry about that. Ferry boats."

Nelumbo abruptly stopped. Tor's eyes went wide, and Nora let out a frightened squeal.

A squad of six mermen and two mermaids armed with spears and tridents surrounded us.

"Where is the princess Kamoana?" asked a merman with a pinkish face and barbels on his chin. "I am Captain Mullet, S.P.L.A.S.H. team leader. King Grouper of Begaia sent us at the request of the great *sahira* Queen Pukai to aid in the rescue of Prince Pike of Onterrica."

"Greetings," I said with a royal nod. "I am Princess Kamoana, Queen Pukai's daughter, and these are my companions, Lord Magnussen and Miss Rachid. They are Prince Pike's friends too."

"Your Highness." He bowed to me, ignoring my companions.

"What is a splash team?" Tor asked. "I'm guessing it's an acronym for some kind of commando force—"

"Law enforcement, not military. We patrol our own surf, not foreign waters," Captain Mullet answered, his voice expressing no emotion. "Special Patrol Liaison Agents for the Security of the Homewater. Our specialty is interspecies conflict, most often human-mer situations."

Eight sets of eyes regarded us with detached stares, and there was a brief silence before Tor responded. "Got it. Thanks."

"Have you located Prince Pike?" I asked.

"Yes, he is there." Mullet used his trident to point toward the ships Tor had identified as ferries. "The second ship from the left, the one with a streak of rust down its side. He is in a room on the starboard side, next to the dock, and he is frightened."

Nora made a sad little sound.

"They sneaked him aboard nearly an hour ago," Mullet continued. "Eight humans: one female, seven males."

"We must hurry to purchase tickets and board the ship," Tor said. "There's no time to lose. When we're ready to move in and rescue the prince, Princess Kamoana will notify you."

Mullet nodded without looking at Tor, held my gaze for an instant longer, then sank beneath the waves.

Tor gave me a sharp look. "You trust them?"

"Yes. They will help us rescue Pike."

He didn't answer, but I read doubt in his face, and I couldn't blame him. The captain had been rude.

As Nelumbo swam on, Nora looked over her shoulder to address me. "I've never seen a merman before," she said, wide-eyed. "They are rather magnificent and frightening, aren't they? What does Pike look like in his true form?"

"Kind of like a pike fish. He is considered extremely handsome by most sirens."

She tried to smile. "No wonder he's so vain. I just hope he's all right. Getting fooled and captured like this might decimate his ego!"

Tor and I shared a glance. Nora hadn't yet seen Pike's cold-eyed fish head, but the description of it hadn't seemed to faze her.

Was my ability to detect Pike's magic still blocked? Mother had grudgingly returned some of my magic that morning, but I hadn't yet tested its limits. We might have to work without magic and simply ask questions once we got aboard the ship.

Nelumbo swam as close to shore as he could, and we stepped from his neck to the top of a rock. "Please stay near the ship so you can hear me call," I asked the serpent. He wiggled his ears and showed those terrifying teeth in his familiar grin as he sank beneath the surface.

"Was that an agreement?" Nora asked.

"I think so. He won't forget about us." Although he might be distracted. For all I knew, dozens of lovely female sea serpents lived in the area. Or he might find any number of other distractions I couldn't imagine.

We had to jump from rock to rock with great care, since there were a few wide gaps between them and some were slippery. Since I was the shortest of the bunch and still unsteady on my feet, Tor had to catch me by the arm more than once to keep me from falling.

At last we reached a strip of pebbled land beneath a steep cliff. An indistinct path led between rocks in the direction of the harbor, and small waves lapped at the shore. Tor dropped his bag in a sheltered place, opened it, and tossed us each a metal bottle of water. "Keep hydrated."

I caught the bottle, then watched as he emptied his in several gulps and tucked the empty bottle back into the bag. Then he stripped off his wetsuit to reveal wrinkled khaki shorts and a loose button-up shirt. Its color matched his sandy brown hair. Nora and I both watched as he inserted one magazine into a pistol, checked the safety, then slipped the gun into a concealed holster and a wicked-looking knife into a sheath. "There's no time to lose," he reminded us. "I'm going ahead to scout out our route. Hurry." And he walked off with his bag over one shoulder.

Nora and I immediately unzipped our wetsuits. It felt good to get out of that hot rubber, but my clothes were as wrinkled and sweaty as Tor's.

"You really do love him, don't you?" Nora asked while folding her suit into a blobby mass. "Tor, I mean."

"Yes." More with every beat of my heart, it seemed.

"Kinda like, it hurts like a jellyfish sting to imagine being without him?" she prodded.

"Good analogy."

I shoved sunglasses onto my face and a cap onto my head, and Nora did the same.

She paused, then confessed, "I feel like that too. And right now, I don't know for sure whether or not my guy is all right."

This earned her a wide-eyed stare. "You mean Mike? Pike?"

Her lips curled in a wistful smile. "Yeah, both of him."

I concentrated on folding my wetsuit and picked up my swim fins. "I guess I thought you liked him for his looks. I mean, I didn't know you were serious."

"Does it bother you?" she asked with a hint of defensiveness.

"Personally? Not at all. I'm just . . . surprised. I suppose I shouldn't be." Pike always had attracted women like blood draws sharks. I couldn't help wondering where Nora thought this might lead. Pike was the crown prince of his lake kingdom. He couldn't stay in human form even if he wished to.

"I'm not expecting anything from him," she said as if reading my thoughts. "I just want to rescue him and know he's all right. He's so funny and stuck on himself, but underneath he's a sweet guy. No one ever taught him to consider the feelings of other people, so he thinks the world revolves around him."

Not exactly model-husband material, I couldn't help thinking. With our possessions in our arms, we started walking toward the docks.

"Behind all his silly talk, he craves respect and friendship," Nora said. "He may not care about me in a romantic way, but we've become good friends. Maybe because he feels safe to talk with a human girl."

"You are keeping in mind that he . . . doesn't look human?" I asked, just to be sure.

She gave me a frustrated glance. "I'm not stupid. Yes, I was shocked at first, but now I don't care. Do you care that Tor doesn't look merman? Prince Mike's looks attracted me at first, but right now I'm worried sick about Pike. The real person he is inside. I don't care what he looks like, I want him safe."

"I do too," I admitted. "I've known him since we were small fry. He's a good guy, really."

Tor was coming to meet us as we approached the road. "Hurry," he called. "We don't dare miss the boat." We stuffed our swim gear into his bag, which he slung over his shoulder; then he pivoted and walked away. Nora and I frequently had to jog to keep up. He bought three tickets at the kiosk, then we stood in line behind other passengers at the gangway. A few men tried to talk to me, but when Tor loomed behind me with his cold stare, they quickly moved on. The ferry ship was enormous, like a movable island. I saw cars and trucks drive into its back end on a ramp that opened flush with the dock. Amazing! When we reached the front of the queue, Tor showed our tickets and we quickly climbed aboard.

Using a printed diagram of the ship, we moved toward the passenger rooms on the starboard side. Nora and I followed Tor along a metal passage—he had to bend over to keep from cracking his head on the ceiling and various doorways. Even Nora had to duck several times.

In a cramped stairwell, a hand grasped my arm. I gasped, but a quiet voice spoke into my ear: "It's Mullet. Tell your attendants to stop."

Tor and Nora had already turned back to check on me, and Tor's gaze fastened to that webbed hand on my arm. "It's Captain Mullet," I whispered.

Mullet pulled me into a space behind some metal tanks, leaving Tor and Nora to follow. "We boarded earlier and assessed the situation," he said. "Two of the humans, both *hembez,* are in the room with Prince Pike, who is conscious."

"Dr. Benyamina is one of them," I said. "Is she using her magic?"

"She uses it to intimidate the other humans," Mullet said. "Her power is not strong, and the man's is weaker. But six humans bearing firearms guard the hall: two at each end, and two outside the doorway to the room."

"How should we proceed?" Tor asked, his voice nearly a whisper.

The floor and walls vibrated with the deep rumble of engines, and a horn blew. We felt the ship give a jolt and begin to move.

"My two siren scouts are in the water, keeping track of Prince Pike and relaying information to me. Three mermen are at the far end of the hall, including Lieutenant Mallorca. Two are at this end with me. Once we enter the hall there will be minimal cover. Do you carry a firearm?" he asked Tor.

"I do." He quietly drew the pistol and held it pointed at the floor. "It's loaded."

"That will help. You may come with us, but the women . . ." Captain Mullet looked at me and Nora.

"We're coming too," Nora said firmly, and I nodded.

Suddenly we heard gunshots and people screaming. A terrified human woman and a man carrying a child rushed past us and up the staircase. They didn't see Captain Mullet. He beckoned to us, and Tor followed first. I went next, with Nora right behind me. As long as the mermen didn't speak to any humans, I thought, we should be safe from notoriety on the nightly news.

Mullet's feet made no noise on the metal floor, and Tor was nearly as quiet. Nora and I tried hard, but we both kept making little noises. We heard another gunshot along with pinging rebounds, but when we reached the entrance to the hall, two mermen had already subdued the two humans standing guard there and tied them up. Terrified eyes stared at us above their gags.

"Can they see you?" Tor asked.

"No," said one of the commandos, a tall, lean fellow with black and white stripes on his arms. "We never spoke to them, so they never knew what hit them." But he was wrapping his own bleeding arm. "I caught a ricochet. We heard shooting at the other end too. The pair outside the door will be on alert now."

Captain Mullet turned to Tor. "You'd better stay here out of sight until we've got them under control, then we can break down the door and rescue Prince Pike." He then addressed his commandos: "Take those two up and toss them overboard."

We all must have gasped, for the captain immediately explained, "Our siren scouts will keep them safe. Queen Pukai wants the humans alive and unharmed, if possible."

When the mermen returned without the humans, Mullet paused. "No word from the sirens about Mallorca's men, but we must complete the mission now. Our time out of water is running out."

The three commandos hefted their tridents and disappeared into the metal tube that served as a hallway on this ship. Tor stood behind me, and Nora faced us across the opening. Sensing something, I looked up at Tor's grim expression. "What are you thinking?" I asked him. "What's wrong?"

"Something about this isn't right. I understand why Mullet pushed ahead, but the merguys on the other end should be closing in. You two stay here, out of sight; I'm going to do some reconnaissance."

Before we could protest, he was gone. We didn't dare shout after him, so I could only fume silently. "You'd better not get yourself hurt." I aimed my silent admonition at where I thought he might be, back on the upper deck, but he wasn't there.

Nora couldn't meet my gaze. I knew she was worrying about Pike, so I took the opportunity to check on him. "Pike, are you all right?" I focused my call toward that room down the hall.

The only response from the kidnapped prince was a strong sense of *not* all right. He was terrified, but I couldn't know why. "Help is coming," I assured him.

"Hurry!" I urged Captain Mullet and knew he heard me.

"I've got to look," Nora said. "Just a peek."

Both of us peered down the hall and saw the three mermen almost within reach of the two human door guards. Then, a shout came from right behind us, "Holt, they're coming. This way!" Bullets zinged off the walls, some of them reaching as far as our doorway and striking the metal stairs beyond us. I spun around and pressed my back to the wall just as Nora gasped, "Jonathan, no!"

"Hello, pretty siren," said a voice I knew all too well.

23

STANDING MOSTLY IN shadow, Jonathan aimed the pistol at my heart and regarded me and Nora through narrowed eyes. "Thanks for bringing along all those extra merfolk for our men to mow down. We'll have magic aplenty to use and sell once our surgeon does his work. Mike's, yours, and a bunch of fish-headed monsters'. Pick of the crop!"

"You're the monster, Jonathan Howell!" Nora cried.

"What did I ever do to you, that you feel justified in stealing my magic?" I asked in rising fury.

He gave me a dimpled smile then looked me over slowly. "You know, even though she pays me well, I would have dropped Saliha and wrecked her plan if you'd taken me as your lover. But no, you preferred Tor. Really? I know about your teen fling, but you're adults now. Seriously, you'd pick that social dropout over me?"

"Any day of the week," I said.

He laughed. "But don't you have a three-day deadline?

Thought I overheard your little friend Eddi say something to that effect. And unless I'm greatly mistaken, good ol' Tor won't even think about making a move on you for months—if he has any moves, that is. He's a complete loser with women."

Something inside me burned hot. "You know what? Tor may not love me, but when I'm with him I feel safe and respected, and I know he treats other people the same way. He's not out for what he can get. If that means he's a loser with women, give me the losing team every time!"

Jonathan slowly bent toward me, keeping one eye on Nora, and reached out to take my face in his hand. When I recoiled, he grabbed my jaw and jerked my face around. I looked directly into the muzzle of that gun. "Too proud for me, are you?"

My eyes caught movement in the shadows under the staircase, and Jonathan straightened and turned—just in time to grapple with Tor, who knocked the gun from his hand. I cringed when the pistol hit the floor, but it didn't go off. Nora snatched it up. "Come on," she cried. "They've stopped shooting in the hallway. Let's go save Pike!"

She started down the hall. I looked back at Tor and Jonathan, who appeared to be pounding on each other with their fists amid shouted accusations and insults. Tor wasn't using his gun or the knife, but I couldn't guess why.

"Kammy, go with Nora," Tor ordered. He had Jonathan pinned to the wall.

So I ran after Nora, horrified to see two mermen seated on the floor with their backs to the wall, one on either side of the open door, both alive but wounded. One of them was Captain Mullet. "Watch out!" he warned us. "We opened the door, but someone in there has a gun. The guards have all been nullified. Mallorca and others are hauling them out to the sirens."

Nora peered around the doorframe then rushed inside, pistol first. "Drop that knife!" she shouted.

Crouched beside the captain, I cautiously peered inside. Pike, still in his human form, lay strapped down on a table in the middle of the small chamber. He couldn't turn his head, but his eyes rolled to see who had entered. "Nora!" he said, his voice weak.

A man wearing blue scrubs laid his instruments back on a tray and raised his hands. I sensed low-level magic emanating from him.

"Pike!" cried Nora and started toward the table.

"Drop the gun, little niece." It was Dr. Benyamina's smooth voice. A chill trickled down my spine as the woman appeared before me, holding the muzzle of a pistol to Nora's temple. "You see? I can surprise you, little siren," she addressed me with a glance. "I have skill and the drive to succeed, but I need more power to work with. Proceed, Dr. Jennings. I want that magic."

"But madam, I'm not sure I can—"

"Just do it!" she snarled, the smoothness gone. Dr. Benyamina pocketed Nora's gun then turned her chilling gaze on me. "Come in and join the party, little siren. Yes, sit right over there in the corner. You'll be next on the table. Don't even think of running. You do, and I'll kill my niece. She's been nothing but trouble this past year, and then she, my own sister's daughter, actually fell in love with an empty-headed merman. What a disgrace!"

I sat in the place Dr. Benyamina indicated, keeping one eye on that gun and the other open to opportunity. But what good could I do? Dr. Benyamina glanced at the door, and it closed and locked itself. Her magic was limited, and using it visibly drained her, but she knew how to apply it effectively.

The surgeon picked up his instruments again and bent over Pike's thigh, preparing to cut.

Nora cried, "No! Aunt Saliha, you can't do this evil thing! It's monstrous!"

Dr. Benyamina caught her niece's arm and pointed the pistol at the back of her head. "Move again, and I'll put a bullet through your thick skull. One less burden to drag around will be a pleasure."

"Don't hurt her," Pike cried, twisting and thrashing to escape his bonds, his eyes wild with fear, while the surgeon struggled to tighten the straps. "Take my magic. Take my blood and bones—everything you want. You can kill me; just don't hurt Nora!"

"Oh, Pike!" Nora sobbed. "Kammy, why don't you do something!"

Her words jarred me out of a fog. What a fool I was, letting Dr. Benyamina control me with her flimsy magic! I had no weapons, but I was still a siren. Just as the surgeon touched the knife to Mike's flesh, I shouted into his mind, "Stop!"

The man dropped everything and clapped his hands to his head with a howl of pain. The next instant, I aimed my full siren scream into Dr. Benyamina's mind: "Evil human, you will pay!"

When Dr. Benyamina shrieked in agony, Nora turned to pluck the gun from her aunt's hand. But Dr. Benyamina was determined and strong, and she wouldn't let go. As the two wrestled, I focused a screech again, "Drop it, you witch!"

The gun fired as Dr. Benyamina collapsed on the floor, wailing and holding first her head, then her foot. Blood welled between her fingers. "Nora, you shot me!"

"That was *your* finger on the trigger," Nora snarled, and drew the other pistol from her aunt's pocket.

Fists pounded at the door. I rushed over to unlock it. "It's all right, we're safe," I said, pulling it open.

Tor and Captain Mullet rushed in, followed by another merman, who was dripping wet. "Kammy, you're safe?" Tor grabbed me by the shoulders, then crushed me to his chest.

"What happened to Jonathan?" I asked, speaking into his shirt.

"I threw him over the side to the sirens. He's lucky I didn't break his neck for holding a gun to your head." Something in his tone made my heart give a leap. But then I felt a flare of magic behind me. Dr. Benyamina!

Breaking Tor's embrace, I turned quickly, ready to protect him from attack. But Dr. Benyamina, still on the floor, flung her nasty spell at Captain Mullet, who caught it in the webbing of one hand and threw it back. She went rigid, her face frozen in shock, her arm and hand still extended.

"Ignorant *hembez*," Mullet said. "Weak and delusional." He efficiently trapped her wrists in magical cuffs, wrapped her bleeding foot, then—despite the bandage around his own ribcage—slung her over his shoulders and stepped into the hall. "Mallorca is fresh; he'll help you clean up here. I've got to get back in the water. We'll meet you at the Queen's council," he called back. "The water door is just behind the ship."

Lieutenant Mallorca subdued the unresisting surgeon in like fashion, then helped Nora free Pike from the table. "Why didn't you use your own magic to fight back?" the tall officer asked the prince.

"I was drugged before I knew what happened," Pike said. "These criminals are so subtle that not even I suspected their heinous plot." He was unsteady on his feet, his eyes dilated and his face pale, yet he held his head high and accepted Nora's tearful, joyous embrace with evident pleasure.

"You would have sacrificed yourself to save me!" she cried against his chest. "You are the bravest, kindest merman ever to live."

I expected him to agree, but instead he took her face between his human hands and gazed into her eyes. "I love you, Nora Rachid," he said in that beautiful voice of his.

Then his gaze lifted to me, and regret filled his eyes. "Kamoana, I am sorry, but you must learn to accept that Nora is the only woman for me. I hope you can forgive me for breaking our betrothal and move on into your bright future."

Standing there with Tor at my back, his hands on my shoulders, I managed to say with proper solemnity, "I accept your apology, Your Highness, and wish you joy." How that joy was to come about, I had no clue, but my wish was sincere. He was a good-hearted buffoon on the whole.

Mallorca exited with the surgeon over his shoulders, leaving Pike, Nora, Tor, and me in the cabin. A message came over the loudspeaker: "All passengers must return to their cabins and remain until further notice. Do not panic. Everything is under control."

"We've got to get off the ship immediately," Tor said, "before any human in authority realizes what has happened. I already confiscated one camera. The henchmen and Jonathan are all in custody of the S.P.L.A.S.H. agents and ready to transport to Queen Pukai's council chamber."

"Nelumbo, we need you right now!" I called directly to my sea serpent. In my normal voice, I said, "Nelumbo is under the ship. Where should he meet us?"

Tor helped Nora support Pike as we rushed into the blood-spattered hallway. "Port side, midway along the ship."

I relayed this information while running. After being tied up and drugged for so long, Pike was barely able to walk, so when we reached the stairs, Tor threw the prince over his shoulders. Nora and I followed, stumbling a little in the shadows. The ship was poorly lighted, at best.

I was relieved to see daylight ahead, and a moment later we burst onto the deck and rushed to the rail. A man shouted somewhere to our right, but we focused only on the huge, dripping, spiky head rising above the rail. Yellow eyes glinted at us.

"Stop!" cried another man, his voice deep and authoritative. But then he must have caught sight of Nelumbo, for his shout rose into a soprano wail and inarticulate cries.

My serpent opened his mouth in a grin filled with glittering teeth, then turned his head and hooked a few spines over the guardrail. Nora climbed up first, then helped Pike while Tor supported him. Tor helped me up next, then climbed up beside me, his bulky bag over one shoulder. "Ready!" he shouted.

Nelumbo unhooked himself, and we watched the ship rush past. Its horn blew a blast, and several more men rushed to the rail and stared out at us. Other people rushed to the rails, shrieking in fright. There might have been video cameras out, but at that distance, with our caps on, we should be able to remain anonymous. Our sea monster bobbed slightly amid white foam and waves, and we gazed into a setting sun. How could it be evening already? Our rescue adventure had seemed to flash past.

"Whew!" Nora exclaimed. "That was close! Thank you, Nelumbo!"

He wiggled his fleshy ear-things.

"Will you take us to Mother's council chamber, please?"

With a rumble I took as assent, he carefully lowered his head and began to slither over the waves toward the harbor of Santa Cyrilla. I soon glimpsed the water door beneath us. Either Mother or Captain Mullet's people had moved it to open water, well outside the harbor. "Everyone, take a deep breath!" I called.

A rush of water, darkness, the flash of the water door, and we emerged—to my great surprise—from the largest pool inside Mother's council cave. Nelumbo slithered across the stone floor and stopped with a hiss. What seemed like a great crowd of people stood or sat there, all staring at us.

Mother was in her human form, wearing a black robe, her hair in a bun much too neat for the actual mass of her hair. Gorgeous as ever, of course. Six men and women, also clad in official robes, stood near her on the platform, all looking annoyed and uncomfortable. I recognized them as magic-council members. The youngest of them appeared to act as court recorder, for he was busily writing in the air with one finger.

The mermen and siren commandos lined nearby pools, while the two abductors and their henchmen huddled together on the floor in abject terror.

It suddenly hit me that this—not a romantic kiss, not a tragic yet poignant denouement, but *this*—was the anticlimax of my three-day test. After working through the important drama of

Pike's abduction and its aftermath, Mother would simply send Tor away and ordinary life would resume . . . for everyone but me.

And Nora.

Nelumbo waited—his back half still in the pool—while we all climbed off, then he wiggled his ears at me and snorted like a foghorn. Every eye in the room turned to him, and he showed his myriad teeth, enjoying the attention.

"Out, you overgrown sea snake," Mother said with a wave of one hand, and Nelumbo vanished. Just as well, I thought. He was far too large to back out of that pool.

Now the anticlimax could begin.

2 4

"ARE YOU TRULY the son of King Burbot of Onterrica?" a short, bearded magician asked Pike.

"Yes, I am Prince Pike," he answered, sounding tired and slightly belligerent, his arm wrapped around Nora—at least partly for support. "Who are you?"

"Your Highness," said my mother, "you are welcome to my home, but I must ask you to address my colleagues with the proper respect." She proceeded to name the men and women standing near. "They are all members of the magic council, the highest governing body in the magical world."

Pike looked unimpressed. "Never heard of any of them. I have an important request to make."

"Later." Mother studied him and Nora, turned a baffled gaze upon me, and asked, "What has happened to Pike? I mean, aside from being kidnapped."

"He can tell you that better than I could. What do you plan to do with her?" I pointed at Dr. Benyamina. "She is the ringleader of the kidnappers who planned to appropriate Pike's magic by stealing his bone marrow. Would that even work?"

Ignoring my question, Mother stalked toward the huddled villains. Cringing in evident dread, Dr. Benyamina watched her approach.

"A *hembez* of minor ability," the queen observed. "Are you licensed, madam? Be truthful. The registry is easily checked and lies will not improve your future."

"I am not," Dr. Benyamina said, her sultry voice now sounding ragged. "I had no one to train me in magic use, so I trained myself."

"Practicing magic without proper authorization is the first charge against you, the abduction of a royal prince is second, and attempted misappropriation of magical essence from a sentient being—incidentally a royal prince of the merfolk—is third. You will be sent to the magic council for trial."

Mother looked to the council members. "I do hope you're recording all this in proper legal terms, Cristobal." The man writing with his finger in the air nodded absently. Mother scanned the other enchanters. "Do any of you have questions to ask or observations to add?"

They all shook their heads. I gave a little sniff. Easy to see who ran the world's greatest political body.

Mother turned upon the doctor a stare that visibly struck dread into the woman's soul. "The council will discover everything." She made a plucking motion with two fingers, and Dr. Benyamina visibly aged by at least ten years. Mother wound up the spell then tossed it to a council member. "Keep this for the trial, Doreen. I'm guessing the magic came from non-sentient magical sources."

"I'll cooperate in exchange for mercy," Dr. Benyamina pled.

"You'll have a fair trial, don't worry," Mother said. "Take her away, Doreen, before the temptation to punish first and question later overcomes me. Make sure she receives necessary medical care."

A grim-faced councilwoman stepped forward to grip the doctor's arm, gave Mother a nod, and the two women vanished.

"Kamoana, list the crimes of these men." Her gaze fell upon Jonathan, who cringed.

"That one is Dr. Benyamina's accomplice," I said. "He was complicit in the abduction. The others are all hired muscle. I'm not certain they even knew what they were protecting."

"Simple enough." Mother spread one hand flat and slowly moved it above the heads of all six terrified hired guns. One after another, they closed their eyes and slumped into peaceful slumber. "Return them to Santa Cyrilla, each to a different location, and they can find their way home."

"But they are criminals, madam," said a councilman.

The queen shrugged one slender shoulder. "Let the mortal police punish them for crimes against mortals. Each of them will have a horror of the sea and magical creatures from now on."

"They shot four members of my team, Your Majesty," Captain Mullet said. "Including me."

Mother's brows rose. "Oh. That makes a difference. They are subject to Council Law for harming magical beings. But what about this one?" She looked down upon Jonathan. "What was your role in this crime?"

Facing the gorgeousness that was Queen Pukai, Jonathan scrambled to his feet, cleared his throat, and spoke in a near falsetto that gradually settled into his usual honeyed tones: "I am Dr. Benyamina's assistant, a friend to Lord Magnussen and Nora

Rachid, and a graduate student at the University of Barbacha. I didn't know about Saliha's plan to steal magical bone marrow until yesterday. The doctor talked me into this whole thing, and I was over my head before I realized what was going on. I find the whole idea appalling and barbaric." With his big brown eyes he gave me a puppy-dog look. "I wouldn't have shot you, Kamoana—I've never shot anyone."

Unfortunately for him, this plea brought back a clear memory of his face and voice when he pointed a gun at my face. "He's lying, Mother. He was complicit in Dr. Benyamina's plans."

She pursed her lips, nodded, and turned to the remaining council members. "Three of you escort these human criminals to the holding chambers then notify the full council that a trial must be held within ten days. Jonas, I leave it to you to notify the proper human authorities. It should be straightforward enough."

Three men stepped forward, divided up the prisoners among them—one added Jonathan to his two sleeping henchmen—motioned as if casting nets over their charges, and vanished. My last glimpse of Jonathan was his hate-filled glare. No dimples.

The air seemed easier to breathe once the villains were gone. Even the remaining council members looked more relaxed.

Queen Pukai turned next to Captain Mullet, Lieutenant Mallorca, and the rest of the commandos, who, at a sharp word from their captain, snapped upright to stand or swim at attention. Mother's brows lifted in surprised approval. "I overlooked the bandages earlier and certainly would not have guessed that any of you had been shot today."

"None of us are seriously injured, ma'am," Captain Mullet said.

She nodded. "Most fortunate. I am indebted to you all and to King Grouper," she said. "Your team extracted the prince safely, apprehended every criminal, and sustained no serious injuries. You performed well, and I will send a special recommendation to your superiors."

Mullet bowed low despite his injury. "Serving you is an honor, Your Majesty. You need to know that your daughter and the two humans played key roles in the rescue, ma'am."

"Did they?" She seemed surprised.

"I doubt the rescue would have succeeded without them," the captain continued. "Lord Magnussen single-handedly disarmed and subdued the accomplice, Miss Rachid prevented injury to the prince, and Princess Kamoana took down the woman and the surgeon with focused siren screams."

"Indeed!" Mother's gaze drifted from my face to Tor's to Nora's. I couldn't read her expression, but she seemed strangely pleased.

My heart swelled with pride in my friends and my people. The S.P.L.A.S.H. team was impressive—fearless, intelligent, and efficient. The siren agents were professional and tough as well as gorgeous. Some of the male agents were handsome mermen, and all were strong and masculine.

But so was my human. I looked up at Tor. Love made him the finest of all in my eyes.

"Thank you all for rescuing me." Pike spoke with more humility than I'd expected from him. "And thanks especially to Kamoana for saving Nora. I won't forget it."

Captain Mullet bowed. "We are honored to have been of service, Your Highness," he said in his deep voice, and the team murmured agreement. The two sirens kept sneaking glances at Prince Pike, trying to hide their fascinated horror. I wondered if they had attended the Siren Song Ball. How strange he must appear to their eyes in his human shape!

Mullet then turned to Tor and me. "We were also honored to serve Princess Kamoana and to work side by side with her human consort, Lord Magnussen." He bowed again and thumped his right fist to his left shoulder in salute. The entire team followed suit.

I barely stopped my mouth from dropping open. They called Tor my consort! What would Mother make of that?

"The honor was mine to serve alongside you," Tor responded with a dignified nod.

I managed to smile and said, "Thank you all." My voice sounded stronger than I had expected, and the eight agents responded with bows.

Then Tor stepped forward and shook hands with each member of the team. I followed a step behind and did the same. The sirens regarded us with friendly curiosity instead of the disdain I had expected, and the mermen were deferential and courteous to both of us.

They then turned to face Mother. With another brief word of thanks, she sent them home in one sweep of her arm. "Handled with utmost efficiency, Your Majesty," the sour-faced council member began in a servile tone, but Mother cut him off.

"Thank you for your prompt response to my summons, Viktor. Thank you for recording events, Cristobal. I will return Prince Pike and the humans to their proper places. You needn't stay longer."

Cristobal bowed and smiled. Viktor's face went rigid, but in the *sahira* merqueen's council chamber he dared not argue. After formal yet hasty farewells, the two vanished.

Mother swept her gaze across the four of us remaining. "Prince Pike," she said, her tone chilly. "If you are fully recovered, step forward alone."

Pike bowed slightly then wrapped his arm around Nora's shoulders. "Begging your pardon, Your Majesty, but Nora comes with me."

Queen Pukai did her best to accept this statement with grace. "It is I who must beg your pardon, Your Highness, for endangering your life, and apparently to no purpose. I fully intended to honor the betrothal agreement, but my plans went sadly awry. I never thought my daughter and this human male would pass the test. If you are ready to return home, I will send you directly."

Pike shrugged one shoulder. "I asked you to make me human, and I have no regrets. I'm not ready to return to Onterrica yet."

I shook my head in frustrated surprise and interrupted: "Mother!"

Mother's gaze moved from Pike to me. "Kamoana?"

"Tor and I did not pass the test. We didn't break the spell." How could she not know? She must know.

She held my gaze for a moment and, for the first time in memory, I saw a shadow of guilt and regret in her eyes. "Ahem. Yes. Your part of the spell is mostly dissolved—you possess more magic than you realize, child—but the young man's memory block is still in place. Why have you not kissed him?"

I spoke in short, angry, painful bursts. "He didn't want to kiss me. He doesn't remember that he loves me."

Mother rolled her eyes and made a clucking noise. I barely managed to contain my wrath as she approached Tor and looked him up and down. "He is tall, strong, and masculine, though not particularly handsome for a human."

Tor's irked expression might have amused me at any other time, but Mother was still talking: "Pike is stunning in either human or merman form, but you've never given him a second look. And he is heir to a vast kingdom, not to a mere grevskab in some cold, northern piece of land. There's simply no accounting for taste. Ah, well."

She spun back to face me and held up three fingers. "I gave you three days to break the spell. You became human at mid-morning Thursday. Your time won't be up until mid-morning tomorrow."

While I digested this information, she pinned Tor with an enigmatic stare and said, "I suggest you kiss my daughter now. That is a verbal suggestion, mind you, not a compulsion."

A rush of hope nearly choked me. I sneaked a glance at Tor. What would he think of this?

His face flushed, but he stood tall, shoulders squared. "I didn't know there was a time limit until Jonathan said so on the ship."

"I couldn't tell you," I said, "and no one else knew it for sure, except Pike."

Nora gave her guy a disapproving stare, and Pike actually looked contrite. "Uh, sorry!"

Tor turned his concerned gaze on me. "What will happen if we break the curse?"

"You will remember everything," my mother said. "If you don't kiss her, you will forget everything about Kamoana. Everything."

"You will steal more of my memories? There should be a law against this," he stated flatly.

Mother blinked. Did I again see regret in her eyes?

Tor turned to me. His feelings were easy to read: fear, embarrassment, frustration, hope. "Are you sure want to try this, Kammy? I mean, I've got nothing to lose in trying and I've got a lot to lose if I don't try, so I'm willing. Just . . . please don't expect too much." His Adam's apple bobbed hard. "All I know for sure is that I don't want to lose you or my memories of you from these past few days."

I struggled to sound calm. "If we don't try, I will always wonder what might have been. And so will you."

Eyes brightening, he took a quick step toward me, then paused and glanced around. "May we have privacy? I—uh—I'm not so good at this sort of thing."

"Neither am I, Tor, but there's nowhere to go that isn't underwater." I walked closer, and his eyes grew wider with every step I took. I stopped in front of him and placed my hands on his solid chest. His shirt was damp with sea water. "I don't know what I'm doing either," I whispered, gazing up into his eyes.

Breathing fast, his hands visibly shaking, he took me by the shoulders, bent his head, and pressed his cool, firm lips to mine. I slipped one hand up to the nape of his neck to pull him down to me and kissed him back. To break Mother's powerful, intricate spell, this had to be more than a casual kiss.

In response, his arms wrapped around me and pressed me so close I could scarcely breathe. I forgot about Mother, about the cave, the spell—everything. I was in Tor's arms at last, and this kiss was real.

25

I FELT THE SPELL break. Everyone in the chamber felt it break. I rather wondered if everyone at Faraway Castle might not have noticed the magical snap.

Then Tor was kissing my cheeks, and my forehead, temples, and ears, murmuring, "Kammy! Kammy, I remember." He trembled from head to toe, and I realized he was weeping. So was I. He hugged me to him, gently rocking me back and forth. "I was like a dead man inside all those years," he spoke into my hair. "Oh Kammy, I've missed you terribly, and I didn't even know it."

I clung to him too. "You broke the curse," I murmured back, still in a daze. "You really do love me!"

"I always did, but that part of me was . . . locked away." He kissed me again, his lips warm and eager. Then his beard brushed my cheek and forehead, and I felt his heartbeat against my face as he pressed my head to his chest. "No more. I'm whole again. Please marry me, Kammy. I don't care if you're mermaid or human, I can't be without you again."

"I will marry you, Tor. Whatever it takes."

"Ahem," my mother said. She had to say it twice before we turned our heads to look at her. Tor did not release me, and I wasn't about to let go of him.

"You two found each other quickly despite having your memories stolen. When you arrived here together, I concluded that the love on both sides was strong enough to shatter my spell, so you required only the kiss. And now—"

Her voice broke off, and she blinked in astonishment. Tor and I turned to follow her gaze and saw Nora holding Pike's face between her hands and kissing him thoroughly. I nearly laughed aloud at Mother's shock.

"Prince Pike!" she exclaimed.

No response.

"Your Highness!"

When Nora let him go, Pike stood there with closed eyes and pursed lips for a few heartbeats, then met Nora's gaze to say, "You are right, my darling. Now I understand the fuss about kissing. In my world only certain gourami fish do it, and it's a form of battle."

Nora rolled her eyes. "Pike, stop talking and kiss me again."

He obediently took her face in his hands, but Mother spoke in a tone impossible to ignore. "Prince Pike."

He slowly turned to look at her. "Your Majesty?" Then his face brightened. "Ah, Your Majesty! I wish to make a request. I asked you to turn me into a human, so I have no complaints on that score. However, if I am expected to keep my father in the dark about how I was abducted and drugged while under your enchantment, I desire something in return. I want to marry Nora."

The succession of expressions flashing across my mother's face was highly entertaining. Her gaze settled on the woman in Pike's firm embrace. "Nora?"

"Yes, ma'am." Nora said with a little wave and her bright smile. "That's me, Nora Rachid, magical-oceanography student. Pleased to meet you, Your Majesty." She looked at me. "You look just like your mother, Kamoana!"

Mother blinked twice, hard, then asked Pike, "You, the crown prince of Onterrica, son of King Burbot and Queen Meoquanee, wish to marry a human?"

He looked down at Nora, lifted her chin with one hand, and gazed into her eyes. "I love you, Nora. Would you marry me?"

Nora's face glowed with happiness. "Yes, Mike. Pike, I mean."

"Are you sure? I won't be able to kiss you anymore. You might not like how I look."

I could hardly believe my ears. Prince Pike feared that Nora might not find him perfectly attractive? Was this the same merman I'd known for years?

"I know. I saw the mermen agents today." She framed his cheek with her palm. "But you'll be you. Besides, I've never kissed anyone until just now, so I won't miss it too terribly!"

Pike's handsome brow wrinkled. "I think I might miss it rather a lot."

Nora again addressed Pukai: "Would you do something to help us, Your Majesty? I'm terribly in love with Prince Pike."

Mother stared as if frozen.

Nora clarified her request. "When you return Pike to his real form, will you turn me into a mermaid?"

Pike stared down at her with awe. "Yes! Nora, you're brilliant!"

"You don't understand what you're asking, Miss Rachid," Mother said, her voice unusually quiet. "You would be living in a world different from anything you've ever known."

"I know, but Pike will be there. I have no human family besides Aunt Saliha, and she's probably going to be in prison for a while. Besides, she kidnapped Mike and drugged me. Not exactly a loving aunt! I'm not so sure she wouldn't have pulled that trigger and killed me to get Pike's magical power. She was crazy!"

"That woman was your relative?" Mother's tone was icy.

I felt Tor's arm tighten on my waist.

"Yes, but she never told me her plan. She knew I would have called the police! Now, I don't know how I'll continue my studies when I'm in mermaid form, but I really don't want to drop out when I'm halfway to getting my master's degree."

I waited for Pike to tell her how she need only be his wife to be content, but he listened with adoration and respect to her every word.

"I can help you with that," Tor volunteered.

Mother shifted her astonished gaze to Tor. "You would help a mermaid complete a degree at a human university?"

"Why not?"

With both arms wrapped around his waist, I rested my head against his chest. He was such a kind and generous man!

My mother observed Tor thoughtfully, gave me a glance, then switched her attention back to Pike and Nora. "You four are shaking up my long-held opinion of human-mer relationships. I offered that three-day trial once before, you see, and the result was quite different."

"I remember your conversation with Madame Genevieve," I blurted. "Is she really your sister?"

Mother nodded. "She never wanted you girls to know. It all happened long ago, when she was very young. Jayachandra begged me to turn her human and was certain she could make that prince love her. All these years she has chosen to retain her human shape rather than face the sympathy or mockery of her fellow sirens."

"How sad!" Nora exclaimed, and I agreed. My opinion of the resort director hadn't changed, yet I better understood her resentment of pretty human girls and any happy romance.

"Had you stolen the prince's memories of her?" I asked.

"He had no significant memories to steal. She rescued him from drowning then left him ashore on the beach beside his palace. He thanked her and promptly forgot about her, but she admired him from afar for weeks. She believed she could make him love her if I would give her just three days in human form."

No wonder my aunt resented my advantages. Tor had loved me before my contest began. "Whatever happened then?" I asked. "Did he marry someone else?" My heart ached for my aunt, imagining how I would feel if Tor had rejected me to wed another.

"It is enough for you to know that her three-day test failed," Mother said curtly, then drew and exhaled a deep breath. "Kamoana and Lord Magnussen, perhaps I was wrong to meddle with your friendship all those years ago, but at the time I believed it was for the best."

I wanted to speak, but Tor gave me a little squeeze and I closed my mouth.

Mother continued: "I desire the best for Kamoana as much as her father, Bluefin, did. I believe he would have been pleased with the baron Lord Magnussen of Hyllestad as our son-in-law." She looked directly at me. "I now agree with him."

I heard Tor suck in sharply. I felt nearly paralyzed with disbelief. Had Mother truly said—

"You will allow us to marry?" Tor asked, still sounding doubtful.

"I shall. You will, I trust, allow your wife to visit her family on occasion. I shall restore her siren form for that purpose, at need."

"Certainly, ma'am." Tor sounded as though the breath had been knocked out of him.

Mother turned to Pike and Nora, who were holding hands. "Prince Pike and . . . Nora . . . You have known each other for a much shorter time. I do not refuse my help, but I advise you, Nora, to try living for a time as a mermaid before you take binding vows."

"Oh, Your Majesty!" Nora gasped, and Pike exclaimed his thanks.

Frowning, Mother studied their smiling faces. "Should you choose to join the merworld and marry Pike, you will be able to regain your human form at will, whenever you desire to continue your studies at university. With help from some of my fellow enchanters, I believe we can work out an arrangement satisfactory to all parties."

Nora gasped with delight, grabbed Pike's gorgeous human face, and kissed him. His amber eyes went wide and round, and he turned to the queen. "When Nora is at her studies in the human world, she will need her husband nearby for protection."

Mother heaved an irritated sigh. "Yes, Pike, you may resume human form whenever you wish. Just please don't tell your father about this whole mess."

A devastating smile brightened his face. "Not a word from me, ma'am. Not a word." With that, he looked at Nora. "Another kiss, if you please."

She gladly complied.

Tor then spoke up. "Ma'am, I should like to visit Kamoana's family and world as well."

I gaped at him. "You would? I mean, you would like to become a merman?"

He gave me a crooked half-smile. "I wouldn't mind giving it a try. I mean, if Pike and Nora can switch back and forth, why can't we?"

I tried to picture Tor as a merman and totally failed. But the idea was intriguing. I turned to my mother, who appeared ready to spontaneously combust, and gave her my best big-eyed entreaty: "Please?"

"I shall consider your request, Kamoana. Do not push me further at present."

I subsided, but I knew she would cave. I just knew it. When she looked away, I gave Tor a quick squeeze and a conspiratorial grin, and he relaxed.

Pike said, "Nora and I have another request, a small one."

Mother looked wary. "What is that?"

"Tonight is the Summer Ball at Faraway Castle, and Nora had agreed to be my date, which seems to be the human word for dance partner. My abduction interfered with our plans, but if we hurry, we might make it back in time for a few dances. Would you—"

"Would I provide you with proper attire and whisk you back in time to enjoy the festivities?" Mother sighed and shrugged her slim shoulders. "Why not?" She then turned to me and Tor. "You two as well?"

I knew how Tor despised dancing, but to my surprise he nodded. "I'm game. Are you, Kammy?" He met my stare of disbelief and laughed. "Dancing at a ball with you sounds like fun, which is a first for me."

"I don't know how to dance with feet," I admitted.

"Neither do I. We'll both do our best not to step on each other. Deal?"

"Deal!"

We turned to Mother and nodded. "Yes, please!"

Mother deposited the four of us under the portico beside the lake, outside the lobby. Two brownies and Sten the dwarf saw us appear, but they merely smiled in relief. "Welcome back! We wondered if you all would make it in time for the party."

I turned to Tor, and my jaw dropped. He looked incredibly good in a tux, his short hair smoothly combed for once, his beard trimmed short. He was too busy staring at me to notice his own attire. "Kammy, I am the luckiest man on the planet. In all history. You're . . . You're beyond-words-beautiful!"

I looked down at myself and nearly laughed. Mother had created a costume as much like the outfit I'd worn to the Siren Ball as a human ballgown could be, shimmery and sheer in places, yet entirely appropriate for the occasion. It was blue and iridescent and quite glorious.

Nora's gown was red satin trimmed in jet beads, and with her hair in flowing curls she looked amazing. Mother truly did know how to match a woman with her best style and colors. Pike, of course, looked too handsome to be real, but for once his good looks didn't annoy me. He made Nora happy, and she made him bearable.

"Shall we?" Tor offered his arm, and I laid my gloved hand in the crook of his elbow.

I thought we might create a sensation, entering late after being gone all day long, but apparently other events had occurred that outshone our entry. It took us a while to get the full story, but eventually we understood that the lifeguard named Ellie—the one who had taken Tor off the island earlier in the week—was actually the long-lost crown princess of a country called Auvers. By Tor's reaction, I gathered that this was astounding news.

As soon as we reached the ballroom, Tor swept me onto the dance floor. Other people wisely kept their distance as we attempted a waltz. I saw Eddi dancing, and Beatrice, who looked lovely and genteel, as always. When she caught sight of me, I gave her a thumbs-up and saw her mouth drop open in amazed delight. As soon as the song ended, both Beatrice and Eddi abandoned their partners to converge on Tor and me. We gladly related our story . . . rather, Tor stood and smiled while I told the tale.

"I knew it!" Eddi cried. "I knew you would remember in time. Kamoana's just too beautiful and sweet to forget, and you're too smart to forget her for long, magic spell or not." She scanned the room for Pike and Nora. "And Nora gets Mike? Lucky!"

She gave me a hug and was off again with a handsome boy. Eddi seemed to know everyone at the castle.

But Beatrice stayed to chat. "So you heard the news about Ellie the lifeguard?" She caught Tor up on the latest news about people I didn't know. Most of it went over my head, but I was too happy to mind.

Tor soon pulled me back onto the dance floor, and we did our best to dance a two-step without trampling on the people around us. The only worse dancer in the room was Prince Pike, but he and Nora looked as blissfully happy as we did.

As I gazed up into Tor's adoring eyes, I had a sudden flashback to a dance of long ago, my hands clasped in his as we swirled through a sunbeam amid a glittering school of tropical fish in a cave under Palau Kalah.

And now he remembered too.

ONE WEEK LATER, Tor and I stood before the resort's chaplain on the beach at Faraway Castle and took our vows. He slipped his grandmother's wedding ring, no longer on its gold chain, onto my finger, and we became husband and wife.

It would seem impossible to put together a wedding on such short notice, but with my mother to handle the couture and brownies to tackle the cuisine, Tor's parents had only to invite their closest friends, and Tor asked a few of his friends to join us. My mother planned an underwater reception for us later at the island, so my sisters and their families were content to watch the service from offshore.

The weather was perfect, and most of the castle guests crowded into the portico or watched through tower windows or from boats off shore. In all, our wedding was the event of the season.

Prince Omar had returned for the weekend to be best man, and Prince Pike and a few of Tor's cousins stood beside him. I had a string of attendants: Nora as maid of honor, then Beatrice, Eddi, and Tor's two sisters, Vigga and Nanna. All of them looked beautiful in shimmering blue and green gowns. I had asked my sisters, but none of them would take human shape for even one hour. My own gown was iridescent white, with a veil of priceless lace donated by Tor's grandmother. I carried a bouquet of waterlilies, my favorite flowers.

Mother looked incredibly beautiful; she had been on her best behavior, gracious and regal, all week long. Tor's parents, the greve and grevinde of Hyllestad, clearly found her overpowering, but they remained cordial throughout, though I know I was hardly their first choice as daughter-in-law. However, as Tor reminded me, they had feared he would never marry, so a princess—even a mer princess—added to the family tree came as a pleasant surprise. Tor's little sisters thought I was the best sister-in-law ever and drank in the story of our romance as many times as they could convince me to tell it until, at last, I thought I had better write it all down to save time.

Madame Genevieve did not attend, which saddened me a little. Mother advised me to give my aunt time to adjust and accept. I hope she will someday heal and maybe even find true love.

We ate cake and ice cream afterward, and then Tor, Pike, Nora, and I sneaked inside to change into ordinary clothes. It was nearly time for our underwater reception. Soon Tor would take on merman form for the first time!

Nora and I changed in my guestroom, glad for the chance to chat in private. "That was the loveliest wedding I've ever seen,"

Nora gushed as she pulled on blue jeans. "Probably because you and Pike were in it. I hope mine will turn out half as nice. We'll be married next month, at court in Onterrica, of course, but Pike wants to have a double honeymoon—one underwater and one on land. We're hoping you and Tor will stand . . . swim . . . um, will be our witnesses."

"I would be honored, and I know Tor will agree." I carefully hung up my gown and smoothed its folds. "We're headed to a South Sea island resort tonight," I confided. "Mother already sent our luggage ahead. But first, our underwater reception! Tor hasn't yet tried out his merman form. I can hardly wait to see it today!"

The party on the beach was winding down for the evening and most of the non-magical guests had already left the resort for their hotels when Nora and I met our guys in the lobby and stepped outside to cheers and a shower of flower petals. Pike and Nora jumped off the dock beside the portico and instantly switched into their mer forms. I heard a few gasps and screams among the wedding guests, but in general everyone seemed intrigued.

"Woohoo!" cried Nora as she surfaced. Her tail was vivid green, and her wrap top matched. Her black hair held natural golden sparkles. Pike's fishlike head and spotted green shoulders appeared beside her, and they both pointed at Tor and me.

"Hurry up, you two!" the novice mermaid cried. She'd studied mer etiquette and traditions all week long and practiced changing form until it no longer hurt at all. She took to mer ways naturally and thought Pike's merman form possibly even more attractive than his human form. Even my mother agreed that Nora seemed born to be Queen of Onterrica.

Tor gave me a hangdog look. "Could we walk over to our place? I really don't want to have an audience the first time I change."

"If you hadn't procrastinated all week, this wouldn't be such a big deal today," I chided him gently but took him by the hand, and we headed toward the running trail. Within a few minutes we stepped off the trail, and I led him down to the water's edge, where we both removed our shoes and stashed them in our old hiding place.

Soon we stood hand in hand on the rocky bank, looking out over the mossy rock where, long ago, we had chatted like any two teenagers and become friends.

"Don't worry. It will be fun," I said. "Remember, even if you hate your looks as a merman, no one else will. All the guys look like fish. And no matter what you look like, you'll still be Tor, not Halibut or Guppy or Clownfish." He smiled rather grimly. I patted his arm. "We shouldn't be late to our own wedding reception, though I suppose everyone would understand. Are you ready?"

"As ready as I'll ever be, I guess." He lifted my hand and admired the ring on my finger. "This looks so good. I never dared hope this day would come."

He wrapped me in his arms and kissed me again. How good it was to realize that Tor was now my husband! How lovely to kiss him and be with him always! I was not only a mer princess now but also the wife of a human baron. No one—not even Mother—would dare try to part us again.

"I suppose we'd better get on with this," Tor said, holding my shoulders. "I just wanted to kiss my wife while I still can." He gave me a sly grin. "But who knows? I might turn into a gourami man, complete with kissing lips!"

Laughing, I slipped from his grasp and ran down into the water. Once I was waist-deep, I felt the magic flow over me. This time the transition was slightly uncomfortable but not painful. I flicked my familiar tail and dove under, then surfaced to watch my new husband undergo his change.

Just as he waded in, something bumped my arm. "Fathoms! Did you see our wedding? Look at Tor—he's going to be a merman soon!"

My catfish purred approval as I scratched around his gills.

The expression on my husband's face defied description— fright, curiosity, then shock. He ducked under the surface before the change was complete, and I saw him swim past. I ducked under, overjoyed to once again breathe the fresh water of my childhood home.

Tor swam up to me, and my mouth dropped open. He was so handsome! Mostly black, but with brilliant red down his neck and chest, and flashes of silver on his arms. He studied as much of his body as he could see, then his round eyes regarded me with blended dread and interest. "Am I an arctic char?"

"Yes," I cried in delight. "One of the handsomest fish in the world!"

He hovered easily in the water, breathing with his gills as if he'd been born to it. A lifetime of swimming served him well in this new form. Fathoms bumped his head into Tor's spotted side, and a large webbed hand reached out to stroke the catfish's back.

I couldn't read Tor's fish face, so I asked, "Are you upset? Did you hope to be a shark or a barracuda or something?"

"No, I'm thankful not to be a wolf eel or a mola mola, and I'm glad you think I'm handsome. But . . . I've caught and eaten an awful lot of arctic char over the years."

"Don't worry. No one will be angling for you at the reception," I assured him. "I've already caught you, and I have no intention of throwing you back."

I took his hand, and we swam to Palau Kalah, into our new life. Together.

THE END

Can Rosa protect the sleeping princess from the infuriatingly charming and dangerously powerful Prince Briar? Find out in Faraway Castle Book 3—

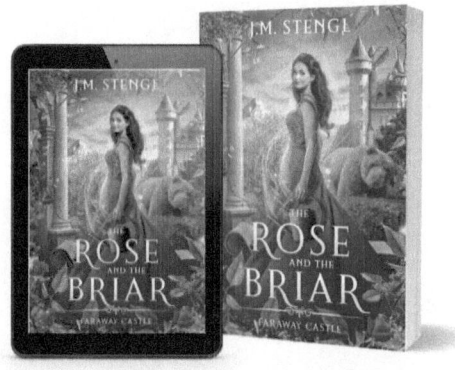

THE ROSE AND THE BRIAR

A Sleeping Beauty Romance

ABOUT THE AUTHOR

JILL MARIE STENGL is a native of southern California who, after a whirlwind life as a military wife, now makes her home with her husband in North Carolina, where she serves at the beck and call of two cats and five adorable grandchildren. Obsessions include all things animal rescue, fairy-tale romances, collecting model horses, and perfecting the perfect pastry crust.

During her former career as a romance novelist, Jill Marie won both the Carol Award and RWA's Inspirational Readers' Choice Award. Now she prefers her novels to include a dash of magic along with the heart-melting romance.

Visit her website at www.JMStengl.com